WITHDRAWN

Contents

Sadeq Hedayat: His Life and Works

S ADEQ HEDAYAT WAS BORN on 17th February 1903 and died on 9th April 1951. He was descended from Rezaqoli Khan Hedayat, a notable nineteenth-century poet, historian of Persian literature and author of *Majma' al-Fosaha*, *Riyaz al-'Arefin* and *Rawza al-Safa-ye Naseri*. Many members of his extended family were important state officials, political leaders and army generals, both in the nineteenth and twentieth centuries.

Hedayat is the author of *The Blind Owl*, the most famous Persian novel both in Iran and in Europe and America. Many of his short stories are in a critical realist style and are regarded as some of the best written in twentieth-century Iran. But his most original contribution was the use of modernist, more often surrealist, techniques in Persian fiction. Thus, he was not only a great writer, but also the founder of modernism in Persian fiction.

Having studied at the exclusive St Louis French missionary school in Tehran, Hedayat went to Europe, supported by a state grant, spending a year in Belgium in 1926–27, a year and a half in Paris in 1928–29, two terms in Reims in 1929 and a year in Besançon in 1929–30. Having still not finished his studies, he surrendered his scholarship and returned home in the summer of 1930. This provides a clue to his personality in general, and his perfectionist outlook in particular, which sometimes resulted in nervous paralysis.

Back in Tehran, Hedayat became the central figure among the *Rab'eh*, or Group of Four, which included Mojtaba Minovi, Bozorg Alavi and Mas'ud Farzad, but had an outer belt including Mohammad Moqaddam, Zabih Behruz and Shin Partaw. They were all modern-minded and critical of the literary establishment, both for its social traditionalism and intellectual classicism. They were also resentful of the literary establishment's contemptuous attitude towards themselves, and its exclusive hold over academic posts and publications.

In the early 1930s, Hedayat drifted between clerical jobs. In 1936 he went to Bombay at the invitation of Sheen Partaw, who was then an Iranian diplomat in that city. Predictably, he had run afoul of the official censors, and in 1935 was made to give a pledge not to publish again. That was why when he later issued the first, limited edition of *The Blind Owl* in Bombay, he wrote on the title page that it was not for publication in Iran, predicting the possibility of a copy finding its way to Iran and falling into the hands of the censors.

During the year in Bombay, he learnt the ancient Iranian language Pahlavi among the Parsee Zoroastrian community, wrote a number of short stories and published *The Blind Owl* in fifty duplicated copies, most of which he distributed among friends outside Iran.

He was back in Tehran in September 1937, although he had returned with great reluctance and simply because he did not feel justified in continuing to depend on his friend's hospitality in Bombay. In 1939, he joined the newly founded Office of Music as an editor of its journal, *Majelleh-ye Musiqi* (*The Music Magazine*). It was literary work among a small group of relatively young and modern intellectuals, including Nima Yushij, the founder of modernist Persian poetry. He might well have regarded that as the most satisfactory post he ever had.

It did not last long. After the Allied invasion of Iran and abdication of Reza Shah in 1941, the Office of Music and its journal were closed down, and Hedayat ended up as a translator at the College of Fine Arts, where he was to remain till the end of his life. He also became a member of the editorial board of Parviz Khanlari's modern literary journal *Sokhan*, an unpaid but prestigious position. Even though the country had been occupied by foreign powers, there were high hopes and great optimism for democracy and freedom upon the collapse of the absolute and arbitrary government. The new freedom – indeed, licence – resulting from the Reza Shah's abdication led to intense political, social and literary activities. The modern educated elite were centred on the newly organized Tudeh party, which was then a broad democratic front led by Marxist intellectuals, although by the end of the '40s it had turned into an orthodox communist party. Hedayat did not join the party even in the beginning, but had sympathy for it and had many friends among Tudeh intellectuals.

But the party's support for the Soviet-inspired Azerbaijan revolt in 1946, which led to intense conflicts within its ranks, and the sudden collapse of the revolt a year later, deeply upset and alienated Hedayat from the movement. He had always been a severe and open critic of established Iranian politics and cultural traditions, and his break with radical intellectuals made him a virtual émigré in his own land. This was a significant contribution to the depression he suffered in the late 1940s, which eventually led to his suicide in Paris in 1951.

For some time his close friend Hasan Shahid-Nura'i, who was serving as a diplomat in France, had been encouraging him to go to Paris. There were signs that his depression was deepening day by day. He was extremely unhappy with his life in Tehran, not least among intellectuals, many of whom were regularly describing him as a "petty-bourgeois demoralizer", and his work as "black literature".

Through his letters to friends one may observe, not far underneath the surface, his anger and despair, his acute sensitivity, his immeasurable suffering, his continuously darkening view of his own country and its people, and his condemnation of life. Through them, perhaps more than his fiction, one may see the three aspects of his predicament: the personal tragedy, the social isolation and the universal alienation.

In a letter which he wrote in French to a friend in Paris four years before his last visit, he had said:

> The point is not for me to rebuild my life. When one has lived the life of animals which are constantly being chased, what is there to rebuild? I have taken my decision. One must struggle in this cataract of shit until disgust with living suffocates us. In *Paradise Lost*, Reverend Father Gabriel tells Adam "Despair and die", or words to that effect. I am too disgusted with everything to make any effort; one must remain in the shit until the end.

Ultimately, what he called "the cataract of shit" proved too unbearable for him to remain in it till the end.

Hedayat's fiction, including novels, short stories, drama and satire, written between 1930 and 1946, comprises *Parvin Dokhtar-e Sasan* (Parvin the Sasanian Girl), *Afsaneh-ye Afarinesh* (The Legend of Creation), '*Al-bi'tha(t) al-Islamiya ila'l-Bilad al- Afranjiya*' (Islamic Mission to European Cities), *Zendeh beh Gur*, (Buried Alive), *Aniran* (Non-Iranian), *Maziyar, Seh Qatreh Khun* (Three Drops of Blood), *Alaviyeh Khanom* (Mistress Alaviyeh), *Sayeh Roshan* (Chiaroscuro) *Vagh-vagh Sahab* (Mr Bow-Vow), *Buf-e Kur* (The Blind Owl), '*Sampingé*' and '*Lunatique*' (both in French), *Sag-e Velgard* (The Stray Dog), *Hajji Aqa, Velengari* (Mucking About), and *Tup-e Morvari* (The Morvari Cannon).

I have classified Hedayat's fiction into four analytically distinct categories, although there is some inevitable overlapping between them: romantic nationalist fiction, critical realist stories, satire and psycho-fiction.

First, the romantic nationalist fiction. The historical dramas – *Parvin* and *Maziyar*, and the short stories 'The Shadow of the Mongol' (*Sayeh-ye Moghol*), and 'The Last Smile' (*Akharin Labkhand*) – are on the whole simple in sentiment and raw in technique. They reflect sentiments arising from the Pan-Persianist ideology and cult which swept over the Iranian modernist elite after the First World War. 'The Last Smile' is the most mature work of this kind. Hedayat's explicit drama is not highly developed, and he quickly abandoned the genre along with nationalist fiction. But many of his critical realist short stories could easily be adapted for the stage with good effect.

The second category of Hedayat's fictions, his critical realist works, are numerous and often excellent, the best examples being '*Alaviyeh Khanom*' (Mistress Alaviyeh) which is a comedy in the classical sense of the term, '*Talab-e Amorzesh*' (Seeking Absolution), '*Mohallel*' (The Legalizer), and '*Mordeh-khor-ha*' (The Ghouls). To varying degrees, both satire and irony are used in these stories, though few of them could be accurately described as satirical fiction.

They tend to reflect aspects of the lives and traditional beliefs of the contemporary urban lower-middle classes with ease and accuracy. But contrary to views long held, they are neither "about the poor or downtrodden", nor do they display sympathy for their types and characters. Wretchedness and superstition are combined with sadness, joy, hypocrisy and occasionally criminal behaviour. This was in the tradition set by Jamalzadeh (though he had more sympathy for his characters), enhanced by Hedayat and passed on to Chubak and Al-e Ahmad in their earlier works.

Coming to the third category, Hedayat's satirical fiction is rich and often highly effective. He was a master of wit, and wrote both verbal and dramatic satire. It takes the form of short stories, novels, as well as short and long anecdotes. They hit hard at their subjects, usually with effective subtlety, though sometimes outright lampooning, denunciation and invective reveal the depth of the author's personal involvement in his fictional satire.

Hajji Aqa is the longest and most explicit of Hedayat's satires on the political establishment. Superficial appearances and critical propaganda notwithstanding, it is much less a satire on the ways of the people of the bazaar and much more of a merciless attack on leading conservative politicians. Indeed, the real-life models for the Hajji of the title were supplied by two important old-school (and, as it happens, by no means the worst) politicians.

Hedayat would have had a lasting and prominent position in the annals of Persian literature on account of what I have so far mentioned. What has given him his unique place, nevertheless, is his psycho-fiction, of which *The Blind Owl* is the best and purest example. This work and the short story 'Three Drops of Blood' are modernist in style, using techniques of French symbolism and surrealism in literature, of surrealism in modern European art and of expressionism in the contemporary European films, including the deliberate confusion of time and space. But most of the other psycho-fictional stories – e.g. *'Zendeh beh Gur'* ('Buried Alive'), *'Arusak-e Posht-e Pardeh'* ('Puppet behind the Curtain'), *'Bon-bast'* ('Dead End'), *'Tarik-khaneh'* ('Dark Room'), *'Davud-e Guzhposht'* ('Davud the Hunchback') and 'The Stray Dog' – use realistic techniques in presenting psycho-fictional stories.

The appellation "psycho-fictional", coined by myself in the mid-1970s to describe this particular genre in Hedayat's literature, does not render the same sense as is usually conveyed by the well-worn concept and category of "the psychological novel". Rather, it reflects the essentially subjective nature of the stories, which brings together the psychological, the ontological and the metaphysical in an indivisible whole.

Hedayat's psycho-fictional stories, such as 'Three Drops of Blood' and 'Buried Alive', which are published together in this volume, are macabre and, at their conclusions, feature the deaths of both humans and animals. Most human beings are no better than *rajjaleh* (rabble), and the very few who are better fail miserably to rise up to reach perfection or redemption. Even the man who tries to "kill" his nafs, to mortify his flesh, or destroy his ego, in the short story 'The Man Who Killed His Ego' ends up by killing himself; that is, not by liberating but by annihilating his soul. Women are either *lakkateh* (harlots), or they are *Fereshteh*, that is, angelic apparitions who wilt and disintegrate upon appearance, though this is only true of women in the psycho-fictions, women of similar cultural background to the author, not those of lower classes in his critical realist stories.

As a man born into an extended family of social and intellectual distinction, a modern as well as modernist intellectual, a gifted writer steeped in the most advanced Persian as well as European culture, and with a psyche which demanded the highest standards of moral and intellectual excellence, Hedayat was bound to carry, as he did, an enormous burden, which very few individuals could suffer with equanimity, especially as he bore the effects of the clash of the old and the new, and the Persian and the European, such as few Iranians have experienced. He lived an unhappy life, and died an unhappy death. It was perhaps the inevitable cost of the literature which he bequeathed to humanity.

Homa Katouzian
St Antony's College and the Oriental Institute
University of Oxford
June 2008

Bibliography

Michael Beard, *The Blind Owl as a Western Novel* (Princeton, NJ: Princeton University Press, 1990)
Nasser Pakdaman, ed., *Sadeq Hedyat, Hashtad-o-daw Nameh beh Hasan Shahid-Nura'i* (*Sadeq Hedayat, Eighty-two Letters to Hasan Shahid-Nura'i*) (Paris: Cheshmandaz, 2000)
Ehsan Yarshater, ed., *Sadeq Hedayat : An Anthology* (Boulder, CO: Westview, 1979)

By Homa Katouzian:
Sadeq Hedayat, His Work and His Wondrous World, ed., (London and New York: Routledge, 2008)
Sadeq Hedayat: The Life and Legend of an Iranian Writer, paperback edition, (London and New York: I. B. Tauris, 2002)
Darbareh-ye Buf-e Kur-e Hedayat (*Hedayat's The Blind Owl, a Critical Monograph*) (Tehran: Nashr-e Markaz, 5th impression, 2008)
Sadeq Hedayat va Marg-e Nevisandeh (*Sadeq Hedayat and the Death of the Author*) (Tehran: Nashr-e Markaz, 4th impression, 2005)
Tanz va Tanzineh-ye Hedayat, (*Satire and Irony in Hedayat*) (Stockholm: Arash, 2003)

Three Drops of Blood

Hajji Morad

(from *Buried Alive*)

HAJJI MORAD SWIFTLY JUMPED OFF the platform of his shop. He gathered about him the folds of his tunic, tightened his silver belt, and stroked his henna-dyed beard. He called Hasan, his apprentice, and together they closed the shop. Then he pulled four *rials* from his large pocket and gave them to Hasan, who thanked him and with long steps disappeared whistling among the bustling crowd. Hajji threw over his shoulders the yellow cloak he had put under his arm, gave a look around, and slowly started to walk. At every footstep he took, his new shoes made a squeaking sound. As he walked, most of the shopkeepers greeted him and made polite remarks, saying, "Hello Hajji. Hajji, how are you? Hajji, won't we get to see you?…"

Hajji's ears were full of this sort of talk, and he attached a special importance to the word "Hajji". He was proud of himself and answered their greetings with an aristocratic smile.

This word for him was like a title, even though he himself knew that he had never been to Mecca. The closest he had ever come to Mecca was Karbala,* where he went as a child after his father died. In accordance with his father's will, his mother sold the house and all their possessions, exchanged the money for gold and, fully loaded, went to Karbala. After a year or two the money was spent, and they became beggars. Hajji, alone, with a thousand difficulties, had got himself to his uncle in Hamadan. By coincidence his uncle died and since he had no other heir all his possessions went to Hajji. Because his uncle had been known in the bazaar as "Hajji", the title also went to the heir along with the shop. He had no relatives in this city. He made enquiries two or three times about his mother and sister who had become beggars in Karbala, but found no trace of them.

Hajji had got himself a wife two years ago, but he had not been lucky with her. For some time there had been continual fighting and quarrelling between the two of them. Hajji could tolerate everything except the tongue-lashing of his wife, and in order to frighten her, he had become used to beating her frequently. Sometimes he regretted it, but in any case they would soon kiss and make up. The thing that irritated Hajji most was that they still had no children. Several times his friends advised him to get another wife, but Hajji wasn't a fool and he knew that taking another wife would add to his problems. He let the advice enter into one ear and come out of the other one. Furthermore, his wife was still young and pretty, and after several years they had become used to each other and, for better or worse, they somehow went through life together. And Hajji himself was still young. If God wanted it, he would be given children. That's why Hajji had no desire to divorce his wife, but at the same time, he couldn't get over his habit: he kept beating her and she became ever more obstinate. Especially since last night, the friction between them had become worse.

Throwing watermelon seeds into his mouth and spitting out the shells in front of him, he came out of the bazaar. He breathed the fresh spring air and remembered that now he had to go home: first there would be a scuffle, he would say one thing and she would answer back, and finally it would lead to his beating her. Then they would eat supper and glare at each other, and after that they would sleep. It was Thursday night, too, and he knew that tonight his wife had cooked sabzi pilau. These thoughts passed through his mind while he was looking this way and that way. He remembered his wife's words, "Go away you phoney Hajji! If you're a Hajji, how come your sister and mother have become something worse than beggars in Karbala? And me! I said no to Mashadi Hosein the moneylender when he asked for my hand only to get married to you, a good for nothing phoney Hajji!" He remembered this and kept biting his lip. It occurred to him that if he saw his wife there and then he would cut her stomach into pieces.

By this time he had reached Bayn ol'Nahrain Avenue. He looked at the willow trees which had come out fresh and green along the river. He thought it would be a good idea tomorrow, Friday, to go to Morad Bak Valley in the morning with several of his friends and their musical instruments and spend the day there. At least he wouldn't have to stay at home, which would be unpleasant for both him and his wife. He approached the alley which led to his house. Suddenly he had the impression that he had glimpsed his wife walking next to him and then straight past him. She had walked past him and hadn't paid any attention to him. Yes, that was his wife all right. Not only because like most men Hajji recognized his wife under her *chador*, but also because his wife had a special sign so that among a thousand women Hajji could easily recognize her. This was his wife. He knew it from the white trim of her *chador*. There was no room for doubt. But how come she had left home again at this time of day and without asking for Hajji's permission? She hadn't bothered to come to the shop either to say that she needed something. Where was she going? Hajji walked faster and saw that, yes, this was definitely his wife. And even now she wasn't walking in the direction of home. Suddenly he became very angry. He couldn't control himself. He wanted to grab her and strangle her. Without intending to, he shouted her name, "Shahrbanu!"

The woman turned her face and walked faster, as if she were frightened. Hajji was furious. He couldn't see straight. He was burning with anger. Now, leaving aside the fact that his wife had left home without his permission, even when he called her, she wouldn't pay any attention to him! It struck a special nerve. He shouted again.

"Hey! Listen to me! Where are you going at this time of day? Stop and listen to me!"

The woman stopped and said aloud:

"Nosy parker, what's it to you? You mule, do you know what you're saying? Why do you bother someone else's wife? Now I'll show you. Help, help! See what this drunkard wants from me. Do you think the city has no laws? I'll turn you over to the police right now. Police!"

Entrance doors opened one by one. People gathered around them and the crowd grew continually larger. Hajji's face turned red. The veins on his forehead and neck stood out. He was well known in the bazaar. A crowd had built to look at them, and the woman, who had covered her face tightly with her *chador*, was shouting, "Police!"

Everything went dark and dim before Hajji's eyes. Then he took a step back, and then stepped forwards and slapped her hard on her covered face, and said, "Don't... don't change your voice. I knew from the very beginning that it was you. Tomorrow... Tomorrow I'll divorce you. Now you've taken to leaving the house without bothering to get permission? Do you want to disgrace me? Shameless woman, now don't make me say more in front of these people. You people be my witness. I'm going to divorce this woman tomorrow – I've been suspicious of her for some time, but I always restrained myself. I was holding myself back, but now I've had all I can take. You be my witness, my wife has thrown away her honour. Tomorrow… you, tomorrow!…"

The woman, who was facing the people, said, "You cowards! Why don't you say anything? You let this good-for-nothing man lay hands on someone else's wife in the middle of the street? If Mashadi Hosein the moneylender were here he would show all of you. Even if I only live one more day I'll take such revenge that a dog would be better off. Isn't there anyone to tell this man to mind his own business? Who is he to associate with human beings? Go away. You'd better know who you're dealing with. Now I'm going to make you really regret it! Police!…"

Two or three mediators appeared and took Hajji aside. At this point a policeman arrived. The people stepped back. Hajji and the woman in the white-trimmed *chador* set out for police headquarters, along with two or three witnesses and mediators. On the way each of them stated his case to the policeman. People followed them to see how the business would turn out. Hajji, dripping with sweat, was walking next to the policeman in front of the people, and now he began to have doubts. He looked carefully and saw that the woman's buckled shoes and her stockings were different from his wife's. The identification she was showing the policeman was all right, too. She was the wife of Mashadi Hosein the moneylender, whom he knew. He discovered he had made a mistake, but he had realized it too late. Now he didn't know what would happen. When they reached police headquarters the people stayed outside. The policeman had Hajji and the woman enter a room in which two officers were sitting behind a table. The policeman saluted, described what had happened, then took himself off and went to stand by the door at the end of the room. The chief turned to Hajji and said:

"What is your name?"

"Your honour, I'm your servant. My name is Hajji Morad. Everyone knows me in the bazaar."

"What is your profession?"

"I'm a rice merchant. I have a store in the bazaar. I'll do whatever you say."

"Is it true that you were disrespectful to this lady and hit her in the street?"

"What can I say? I thought she was my wife."

"Why?"

"Her *chador* has a white trim."

"That's very strange. Don't you recognize your wife's voice?"

Hajji heaved a sigh. "Oh, you don't know what a plague my wife is. My wife imitates the sound of all the animals. When she comes from the public baths she talks in the voices of other women. She imitates everyone. I thought she wanted to trick me by changing her voice."

"What impudence," said the woman. "Officer, you're a witness. He slapped me in the street, in front of a million people. Now all of a sudden he's as meek as a mouse! What impudence! He thinks the city has no laws. If Mashadi Hosein knew about it he'd give you what you deserve. To his wife, your Honour!"

The officer said, "Very well, madam. We don't need you any more. Please step outside while we settle Mr Morad's account."

Hajji said, "Oh God, I made a mistake, I didn't know. It was an error. And I have a reputation to protect."

The officer handed something in writing to the policeman. He took Hajji to another table. Hajji counted the bills for the fine with trembling hands and put them on the table. Then, accompanied by the policeman, he was taken outside in front of the police headquarters. People were standing in rows and whispering in each other's ears. They lifted Hajji's yellow cloak from his shoulders and a man with a whip in his hand came forwards and stood next to him. Hajji hung his head with shame and they whipped him fifty times in front of a crowd of spectators, but he didn't move a muscle. When it was over he took his big silk handkerchief out of his pocket and wiped the sweat from his forehead. He picked up his yellow cloak and threw it over his shoulders. Its folds dragged on the ground. With his head lowered, he set out for home, and tried to set his foot down more carefully to stifle the squeaking sound of his shoes. Two days later Hajji divorced his wife.

Three Drops of Blood

(from *Three Drops of Blood*)

I T WAS ONLY YESTERDAY that they moved me to a separate room. Could it be that things are just as the supervisor had promised? That I would be fully recovered and be released next week? Have I been unwell? It's been a year. All this time, no matter how much I pleaded with them to give me pen and paper they never did. I was always thinking to myself that if I got my hands on a pen and a piece of paper, there would be so much to write about. But yesterday, they brought me a pen and some paper without me even asking for it. It was just the thing that I had wanted for such a long time, the thing that I had waited for all the time. But what was the use? I've been trying hard to write something since yesterday but there is nothing to write about. It is as if someone is holding down my hand or as if my arm has become numb. I'm focusing on the paper and I notice that the only readable thing in the messy scribbling I've left on it is this: "three drops of blood".

* * *

The azure sky; a green little garden; the flowers over the hill have blossomed and a quiet breeze is bringing over their fragrance to my room. But what's the use? I can't take pleasure in anything any more. All this is only good for poets and children and those who remain children all their lives. I have spent a year in this place. The cat's hissing is keeping me awake from night till dawn. The terrifying hissing, the heart-rending mewling, have brought me to the verge of giving up. In the morning, I've barely opened my eyes and there is the rude injection. What long days and terrifying hours I have spent here. On summer days we put on our yellow shirts and yellow trousers and come together in the cellar. Come winter we sit by the side of the garden, sun bathing. It's been a year since I've been living with these weird and peculiar people. There is no common ground between us.

9

I am as different from them as the earth is from the sky. But their moaning, silences, insults, crying and laughter will forever turn my sleep into nightmare.

* * *

There's still an hour left until we eat our supper. It's one of those printed menus: yoghurt soup, rice pudding, rice, bread and cheese, just enough to keep us alive without starving us. Hasan's utmost wish is to eat a pot of egg soup and four hunks of bread. When it's time for him to be released they should bring him a pot of egg soup instead of pen and paper. He is one of the lucky ones here, with his short legs, stupid laugh, thick neck, bald head, and rough hands that look as if they've been made to clean sewers. Had it not been for Muhammad Ali, who stands there inspecting lunch and dinner, Hasan would have sent all of us to God. But Muhammad Ali himself is also just one of the people of this realm. No matter what they say about this place, the fact is that this is a different world to the world of normal people. We have a doctor who, I swear to God, doesn't notice anything. If I were in his place, one night I would put poison into everyone's supper and give them it to eat. Then in the morning I would stand in the garden with my hands on my hips and watch the corpses being carried out. When they first brought me here I was obsessively watching my food, fearing that they might poison me. I wouldn't touch lunch or supper unless Muhammad Ali had tasted the food first. Only then would I eat. At night I would leap awake frightened, imagining that they had come to kill me. How far away and vague that all seems now. Always the same people, the same food, the same room which is blue half way up the wall.

It was two months ago when they threw a lunatic into that prison at the end of the courtyard. With a broken piece of marble he cut out his own stomach, pulled out his intestines and played with them. They said he was a butcher – he was used to cutting stomachs. But that other one had pulled out his own eyes with his own nails. They tied his hands behind his back. He was screaming and the blood had dried on his eyes. I know that all of this is the supervisor's fault.

Not everyone here is like this. Many of them would be unhappy if they were cured and released. For example that Soghra Sultan who is in the women's section. Two or three times she tried to escape but they caught her. She's an old woman, but she scratches plaster off the wall and rubs it on her face for powder. She even uses geraniums to make her cheeks look rosy. She thinks she's a young girl. If she was to recover and look in the mirror she would have a heart attack. Worst of all is our own Taqi, who wants to turn the world upside down. In his opinion women are the cause of men's misfortune, and to improve the world all women must be killed. He has fallen in love with Soghra Sultan.

All this is the fault of our very own supervisor. He is so crazy that he puts the rest of us to shame. With that big nose and those small eyes, like a drug addict, he always walks at the bottom of the garden under the pine tree. Sometimes he bends over and looks under the tree. Anyone who sees him would think what a poor, harmless man to have been caught with all these lunatics. But I know him. I know that there, under the tree, three drops of blood have fallen onto the ground. He has hung a cage in front of his window. The cage is empty because the cat has had his canary. So he has left the cage hanging to lure the cats to the cage and then kill them.

It was only yesterday when he followed a calico cat. As soon as the animal went up the tree towards the window, he told the guard at the door to shoot the cat. Those three drops of blood are the cat's but if anyone asked he would say they belong to the bird of truth.

Stranger than everyone else here is my friend and neighbour Abbas. It hasn't been two weeks since they brought him. He has been warming to me. He thinks he is a poet and a prophet. He says every vocation, but especially that of a prophet, depends on chance and luck. People with high foreheads, for example, have it made even if they don't know much. Whereas those with a short forehead, even if they are the wisest of all men in the world, end up like him. Abbas also thinks he is a skilful sitar player. He has put wires on a wooden board, making himself believe that he's built a string instrument. He also has composed a poem which he recites for me eight times a day. I think it is for the same poem that they sent him here. He has composed a peculiar ballad:

> What a pity that once more it is night.
> From head to toe the world is dark.

For everyone it has become the time of peace
Except me, whose despair and sorrow are increased.

There is no happiness in the nature of the world,
Except death there is no cure for my sorrow.
But at that corner under the pine tree
Three drops of blood have fallen free.

Yesterday we were walking in the garden. Abbas was reciting the same poem. A man and a woman and a young girl came to see him. So far they have come five times. I had seen them before and I knew them. The young girl brought a bouquet of flowers. She smiled at me. It was apparent that she liked me. She had come for me, basically. After all, Abbas's pockmarked face isn't attractive, but when the woman was talking to the doctor I saw Abbas pulling the young girl aside and kissing her.

* * *

Up to now no one has come to see me or brought me flowers. It has been a year. The last time it was Siavosh who came to see me. Siavosh was my best friend. We were neighbours. Every day we went to the Darolfonoun* together and walked back home together and discussed our homework. In leisure time I taught Siavosh to play the sitar. Rokhsare, who was Siavosh's cousin and my fiancée, would often join us. Siavosh wanted to marry Rokhsare's sister but one month before the day of the marriage ceremony, he unexpectedly fell ill. Two or three times I went to see him and to inquire how he was, but they said the doctor had strictly forbidden anyone to speak with him. No matter how much I insisted, they gave the same answer. So I stopped insisting.

I remember that day quite well. It was near the final exams. One evening, I had returned home and had dropped my books and some notebooks on the table. As I was about to change my clothes I heard the sound of a bullet being shot. The sound was so close that it frightened me because our house was behind a ditch and I had heard that there had been robberies near us. I took the revolver from the drawer and went to the courtyard and stood there, listening. Then I

12

went up the stairs to the roof, but I didn't see anything. On my way down from the roof, I turned to look at Siavosh's house from the top. I saw him in a shirt and underpants standing in the middle of the courtyard. I said in surprise, "Siavosh, is that you?" He recognized me and said, "Come over, nobody's home." He put a finger on his lips and with his head he signalled to me to go over to him. I went down fast and knocked on the door of his house. He himself opened the door for me. With his head down and his eyes fixed on the ground, he asked me, "Why didn't you come to see me?"

"I came two or three times to see how you were, but they said that the doctor wouldn't permit it."

"They think I'm ill, but they're mistaken."

"Did you hear the bullet shot?"

He didn't answer but took my hand and led me to the foot of the pine tree where he pointed at something. I looked closely. There were three drops of fresh blood on the ground.

Then he took me to his room and closed all the doors. I sat on a chair. He turned the light on and sat opposite me on a chair in front of the table. His room was simple. It was blue, and up to the middle the walls were a darker colour. In the corner of the room there was a sitar. Several volumes of books and school notebooks had been dropped on the table. After a while Siavosh took a revolver from the drawer and showed it to me. It was one of those old revolvers with a mother-of-pearl handle. He put it in his trouser pocket and said, "I used to have a female cat – her name was Coquette. You might have seen her. She was one of those ordinary calico cats. She had two large eyes that looked as if she had black eyeliner on. The patches on her back were arranged neatly as if someone had spilt ink on a grey piece of blotting paper and then had torn the paper in the middle. Every day when I returned home from school Coquette would run up to me, miaowing. She would rub herself against me and when I sat down she would climb over my head and shoulders, rubbing her snout against my face and licking my forehead with her rough tongue, insisting that I kiss her. It's as if female cats are wilier and kinder and more sensitive than male cats. Apart from me, Coquette got along very well with the cook because he was in charge of the food. But she kept away from my grandmother who was bossy and regularly said her prayers and avoided cat hair. Coquette must have thought to herself that people were smarter than cats and that they had confiscated all the delicious food and the warm, comfortable places for themselves and in order to have a share in these luxuries, cats had to be sycophantic and flatter people a great deal.

"The only time Coquette's natural feelings would awaken and come to the surface was when she got hold of the bleeding head of a rooster. Then she would change, turning into a fierce beast. Her eyes would become bigger and sparkle. Her claws would pop out of their sheaths and with long growls she would threaten anyone who got near her. Then, as if she were fooling herself, she would start to play a game. Since with all the force of her imagination she had made herself believe that the rooster's head was a living animal, she would tap the head with her paw. Her hair would stand up, she would hide, be on the alert, and would attack again, revealing all the skill and agility of her species in repetitive jumping and attacking and retreating. After she tired of this exhibition, she would greedily finish eating the bloody head and for several minutes afterwards she would search for the rest of it. And so, for an hour or two, she would forget her artificial civilization, wouldn't go near anyone and wouldn't be charming or flattering.

"All the time during which Coquette was displaying affection she was in fact secretive and brutish and wouldn't reveal her secrets. She treated our home like her own property and if a strange cat happened to enter the house, especially if the cat was a female, for hours you'd hear the sound of spitting, moaning and indignation.

"The noise that Coquette made to announce that she was ready for lunch was different to the one she made when she was being flirty. The sound of her screams when she was hungry, the cries she made during fighting, and her moaning when she was in heat all had a distinct sound and were different from each other. And their tunes would also change: first there were the heart-rending cries, second the yells of spite and vengeance, third a painful sigh drawn from the natural need to join her mate. The looks that Coquette made with her eyes appeared more meaningful than anything else and sometimes she would display emotions of such human nature that people would feel compelled to ask themselves: what thoughts and feelings exist in that woolly head, behind those green mysterious eyes?

"It was last spring when that terrible incident took place. You know that come spring, all animals become intoxicated and pair up. It is as if the spring breeze awakens crazy passion in all living beings. For the first time our Coquette was hit by the passion of love and, with shudders which moved her whole body, she would sigh with sadness. The male cats heard her sighs and welcomed her from all sides. After fighting and scuffling, Coquette chose for her mate the one who was the strongest of all and whose voice was the loudest. In animal lovemaking their special smell is very important. That's why spoilt, domesticated and clean male cats don't appeal to the females. By contrast, the cats on the walls, the thieving, skinny, wandering and hungry cats whose skin gives off the original odour of their species, are more attractive to the females. During the day, but especially at night, Coquette and her mate would bawl out their love in long cries. Her soft delicate body would writhe while the other's body would bend like a bow, and they would give happy groans. This continued until the coming of dawn. Then Coquette would enter the room with tousled hair, bruised and tired but happy.

"I didn't sleep at night because of Coquette's lovemaking. Eventually, I became very angry. One day I was working in front of this same window when I saw the lovers strutting in the garden. With the very revolver that you see I aimed at them from a distance of two or three steps. I fired the gun and a bullet hit her mate. It seemed as if his back was broken. He made a huge leap and without making a sound or groaning, he ran away through the passageway and fell at the foot of the garden wall.

"Blood had trickled all along the path he had taken. Coquette searched for a while until she found his footsteps. She smelled his blood and went straight to his dead body. For two nights and two days she kept watch by his body. Sometimes she would touch him with her paw as if to say to him, 'Get up, it's the beginning of spring. Why do you sleep in the time of love? Why don't you move? Get up, get up!' Coquette didn't know about death and didn't know that her lover was dead.

"The day after that, Coquette disappeared together with her mate's body. I searched everywhere, I asked everyone for traces of her. It was useless. Was Coquette sulking? Was she dead? Did she go to search for her love? And what happened to the body?

"One night I heard the miaowing of that same male cat. He cried until dawn. The next night was the same, but in the morning his cries had stopped. The third night I picked up the revolver again and I shot aimlessly towards the pine tree in front of my window. The glittering of his eyes was apparent in the dark. He gave a long moan and became silent. In the morning I saw that three drops of blood had fallen onto the ground under the tree. Since that night he's been coming every night and moaning in that same voice. The others sleep heavily and don't hear. No matter what I say to them they laugh at me but I know, I am certain, that this is the sound of the same cat that I shot. I haven't slept since that night. No matter where I go, no matter which room I sleep in, this damn cat moans in his frightening voice and calls for his mate.

"Today when there was no one in the house I went to the same place where the cat sits and cries every night and I aimed, since I knew where he stood from the glitter of his eyes in the dark. When the gun was empty I heard the cat's groans and three drops of blood fell from up there. You saw them with your own eyes, aren't you my witness?"

Then the door opened and Rokhsare and her mother entered the room. Rokhsare had a bouquet of flowers in her hand. I stood up and said hello, but laughing, Siavosh said, "Of course you know Mr Mirza Ahmad Khan better than I do. An introduction isn't necessary. He testifies that with his own eyes he has seen three drops of blood at the foot of the pine tree."

"Yes, I have seen them."

But Siavosh walked towards me, giving a throaty laugh. He put his hand in my trouser pocket and pulled out the revolver. Putting the pistol on the table, he said, "You know that Mirza Ahmad Khan not only plays the sitar and composes poetry well, but he is also a skilled hunter. He shoots very well." Then he signalled to me. I too stood up and said, "Yes, this afternoon I came to pick up some school notes from Siavosh. For fun we shot at the pine tree for a while, but those three drops of blood don't belong to the cat, they belong to the bird of truth. You know that according to legend the bird of truth ate three grains which belonged to the weak and the unprotected and each night he cries and cries until three drops of blood fall from his throat. Or maybe, a cat had caught the neighbour's canary and then the neighbour shot the cat and the wounded cat then passed by the

16

tree. Now wait, I'm going to recite a new poem I have written." I picked up the sitar and tuned it in preparation for the song and then I sang this poem:

"What a pity that once again it is night.
From head to toe the world is dark.
For everyone it has become the time of peace
Except for me, whose despair and sorrow are increased.

There is no happiness in the nature of the world.
Except death there is no cure for my sorrow.
But at that corner under the pine tree
Three drops of blood have fallen on the ground."

At this point Rokhsare's mother went out of the room angrily. Rokhsare raised her eyebrows and said, "He is mad." Then she took Siavosh's hand and both of them laughed and laughed and then walked through the door and closed it on me. From behind the window I saw that when they reached the courtyard they embraced each under the lantern and kissed.

The Legalizer

(from *Three Drops of Blood*)

FOUR HOURS WERE LEFT before the sunset and Pass Qale* looked empty and quiet in the middle of the mountains. Arranged on a table in front of a small coffeehouse were jugs of yoghurt drink, lemonade and glasses of different colours. A dilapidated record player and some scratchy records stood on a bench. The coffeehouse keeper, his sleeves rolled up, shook the bronze samovar, threw out the tea leaves, then picked up the empty gasoline drum, to which wire handles had been attached, and walked in the direction of the river.

The sun was shining. From below could be heard the monotonous sound of the water, layer after layer of water falling on each other in the riverbed, making everything seem fresh. On one of the benches in front of the coffeehouse, a man was lying, a damp cloth covering his face, his cloth shoes arranged side by side next to the bench. On the opposite bench, under the shade of a mulberry tree, two men were sitting together. Though they hardly knew each other they had immediately embarked on a heart-to-heart conversation. They were so absorbed in their conversation that it seemed as if they had known each other for years. Mashadi Shahbaz was thin, scrawny, with a heavy moustache and eyebrows that met in the middle. He was squatting on the edge of the bench, and gesturing with his henna-dyed hand, saying, "Yesterday I went to Morgh Mahale to see my cousin; he has a little garden there. He was saying that last year he sold his apricots for thirty tomans. This year they were frostbitten and all the fruit fell off the tree. He was in a terrible condition. And his wife has been bedridden since Ramadan. It's been very costly for him."

Mirza Yadellah adjusted his glasses, sucked his pipe with an air of relaxation, stroked his greying beard, and said, "All the blessing has gone out of everything."

Shahbaz nodded in agreement and said, "How right you are. It's like the end of the world. Customs have changed. May God grant much luck to everyone – twenty-five years ago I was in the neighbourhood of the holy city of Mashad. Three kilos of butter for less than a rial, ten eggs for a rial. We bought loaves of bread as tall as a man. Who suffered from the lack of money? God bless my father – he had bought a *bandari* mule, they're fast and small, and we would ride it together. I was twenty years old. I used to play marbles in the alley with the kids from our neighbourhood. Now all the young people lose their enthusiasm easily. They turn from unripe grapes to fully-fledged raisins. Give me the days of our youth. As that fellow, God bless him, said:

> I may be old, with a trembling chin,
> But I'm worth a hundred young men."

Yadollah puffed on his pipe and said, "Every year we regret the last year."

Shahbaz nodded. "May God grant his creatures a happy ending."

Yadollah assumed a serious expression. "I'll tell you, there was a time when we had thirty mouths to feed in our house. Now every day I worry about where I'll find a few rials for my tea and tobacco. Two years ago I had three teaching jobs, I earned eight tomans a month. Just the day before yesterday, on Aide Qorban,* I went to the house of one of the wealthy people where I used to be the tutor. They told me to bless the sheep in preparation for the slaughter. The ruthless butcher lifted the poor animal up and threw it onto the ground. He was sharpening his knife. The animal struggled and pulled itself up from under the butcher's legs. I don't know what was on the ground, but I saw that the animal's eye had burst open and was bleeding. My heart was bleeding. I left on the pretext that I had a headache. All that night I saw the sheep's head before my eyes, it was covered in blood. Then a profanity slipped from my tongue and I was having blasphemous thoughts… May God strike me dumb. There's no doubt in God's goodness, but these helpless animals… it's sinful. Oh Lord, oh Providence, you know better. No matter what, man is sinful." He sat lost in thought for a moment. Then he continued, "Yes, if only I could spell out everything that is in my heart: well, but everything can't be said, God forbid. May God strike me dumb."

As if he were bored Shahbaz said, "Just think of important things."

Mirza Yadollah replied with an air of indifference, "Yes, what can we do? The world's always this way."

"Our time is over," said Shahbaz. "We're done for. We're only alive because we can't afford shrouds. What tricks haven't we played in this base world? Once in Tehran I had a grocery store. I put away six rials a day after expenses."

Mirza Yadollah interrupted his words. "You were a grocer? I don't like grocers as a group."

"Why?"

"It's a long story. But you finish what you have to say first."

Shahbaz continued talking. "Yes, I had a grocery store. I was doing all right. Little by little I was building a life for myself. To make a long story short, I married a shrew. It's been five years since my wife ruined my life. She wasn't a woman, she was a firebrand. How hard I had worked to marry and settle down: she ruined everything I had accomplished. Well, one night she came back from listening to a sermon. She insisted that she must go on pilgrimage to lighten her burden of sin. You wouldn't believe how much she harassed me... How silly I was to give my wits to that woman. In any case, man is gullible. I was strong and ruthless, but a woman got the better of me. God forbid that a woman should get under a man's skin. That very night she said, 'I don't understand these things, but I've figured it out. I don't want my dowry back, just set me free. I have a bracelet and a necklace, I'll sell them and leave. I looked for an omen and I found a good one. Either divorce me or I'll strangle your child right here by the lamp.' No matter what I did, do you think I was a match for her? For two weeks she didn't look at me. She insisted so much that I sold everything I had, collected the money and gave it to her. She took my two-year-old son and disappeared to where the Arabs play the flute. It's been five years and I don't know what happened to her."

"May she be protected from the evil of the Arabs."

"Yes, amidst those naked ignorant Arabs, the desert, the burning sun! It's as if she'd turned into water and had been soaked up by the earth. She didn't send me even a note. They're right when they say the woman is made of only one rib."

Mirza Yadollah said, "It's men's fault, they raise them that way and don't let them become worldly and experienced."

Shahbaz was wrapped up in his own words. "What's funny is that that woman was basically silly and simple minded. I don't know what happened that suddenly she turned into a firebrand. Sometimes, when she was on her own, she would cry. I wished her tears were for her first husband…"

"You mean you were her second husband?" asked Mirza Yadollah.

"Of course," replied Shahbaz. "Now what was I saying? I forgot what I was saying."

"You mentioned her first husband."

"Yes, at first I thought she was crying for her first husband. In any case, no matter how nicely I tried to explain and make her understand, it was as if I was talking to a wall. It was as if death were out to get her. I don't know what she did with my son. Will I ever look into his eyes again? A son whom God gave me after so many prayers and offerings."

Mirza Yadollah said, "Everyone you look at has some misfortune. The heart of the matter is that people should be human, should be educated. As long as they behave like mules, we'll ride them. There was a time when I used to preach from the pulpit that whoever made a pilgrimage to the holy shrines would be forgiven and would have a place in heaven."

Shahbaz said, "You aren't a preacher, are you?"

"That was twelve years ago. You see I'm not dressed like a preacher. Now I'm a jack of all trades and master of none."

"How? I don't understand."

Mirza Yadollah moistened his lips with his tongue and said dejectedly, "A woman ruined my life also."

Shahbaz said, "Oh, these women!"

"No, this has nothing to do with women. This misfortune is my own fault. If you were in Tehran, probably you've heard the name of my father. I wasn't found under a cabbage leaf. My father was so holy that even angels obeyed him. Everyone was always extolling his virtues. When he went up to the pulpit, there wasn't even room to drop a needle. All the bigwigs were nervous around him. I'm not trying to show off. He's dead, God bless him. Whatever he was, it was his reputation. As the poet says:

Even if your father was a learned man,
It's nothing to you – you must do what you can.

"In any case, after my father's death I became his successor, and I examined our circumstances. He had left us a house and a handful of stuff. I was still a theology student, and I had a monthly pension of four tomans plus fifteen kilograms of wheat. In addition, during the months of *Muharram* and *Safar* we were in clover. Our bread was buttered on both sides. Since it was well known that the breath of my father, God bless him, would work miracles, one night I was brought to a sickbed to pray. I saw a girl, about eight or nine years old, hanging around. Sir, I was drawn to her at first glance. Well, that's youth, with all its ups and downs.

"Before her I had had two temporary wives, both of whom I had divorced, but this was something else. You'd have to have been me to understand. Anyway, two days later I sent a handkerchief full of nuts and dried fruit and three tomans, and I married her. At night when they brought her, she was so tiny that they carried her. I was ashamed of myself. I won't hide anything from you. For three days, whenever the girl saw me she trembled like a sparrow. Now, I was only thirty, I was in my prime. But talk about those seventy-year-old men with all kinds of diseases who marry nine-year-old girls.

"Well, what does a child understand of marriage? She thinks it's all about wearing a sequinned shawl and putting on new clothes and being patted and caressed by a husband instead of being in her father's house where she would be beaten and cursed. But she doesn't know that life isn't just a bed of roses in her husband's house either.

"In any case, it took me so much trouble to tame her. She was afraid of me. She would cry. I pleaded with her. I would say, 'For God's sake, stop embarrassing me. All right, you sleep at one end of the room, I'll sleep at the other', because I felt sorry for her. I really restrained myself not to force her. Besides, I had had a lot of experience and I could wait. In any case, she listened to my advice.

"The first night I told her a story. She fell asleep. The second night I started another story and left half of it for the next night.

"The third night I didn't say anything, until she finally said, 'You told the story up to the part where King Jamshid went hunting. Why don't you tell the rest?' And I – I couldn't contain myself for joy. I said, 'Tonight I have a headache. I can't talk loud. If you let me, I'll come a little closer.' In this manner I went closer, closer, till she gave in."

Shahbaz was amused. He wanted to say something, but when he saw Mirza Yadollah's serious face and his eyes full of tears behind his glasses, he restrained himself.

With peculiar emphasis Mirza Yadollah said, "That story goes back twelve years, twelve years! You don't know what a woman she was, so nice, so kind. She took care of all my work. Oh, now when I remember... She wore a *chador* all the time. She washed the clothes with her little hands, hung them on the line, mended my shirts and socks, cooked the food, even helped my sister. How well she behaved, how kind she was! She made everybody love her. How clever she was! I taught her how to read and write. She was reading the Koran in two months. She memorized poetry. We were together for three years, the best years of my life. As luck would have it, at that time I became the lawyer for a pretty widow who was wealthy too: well I hankered for her, all right, until it occurred to me that I should marry her. I don't know what scoundrel brought the news to my wife. Sir, may you never see such a day. This woman who was apparently so silly and dumb! I didn't know she could be so jealous. No matter how hard I tried to pull the wool over her eyes with sweet nothings, could I be a match for her? In spite of the fact that the widow owed me part of my fees, I decided not to marry her, and our relationship came to an end. But you don't know what problems my wife created for me for a month!

"Maybe she had gone mad, maybe she'd been bewitched. She had completely changed. She put her hands on her hips and said things to me which one couldn't even imagine. She said, 'I hope you're strangled with your own deceiving turban. I hope to see those spectacles on your corpse. From the very first day I realized you were not my type. May my father's pimping soul burn for having given me to you. Once I opened my eyes I saw I was being embraced by a pimp. It's three years that I've put up with your beggary. Was this my reward? May God spare us from having to deal with unprincipled people. I vow not to make a mistake like this again. You can't force me. I don't want to live with you any more. I don't want my dowry back, just let me go. I swear I'll go, I'll go and take sanctuary. Right now. Right now.'

"She said so much that I finally felt infuriated. Everything went dark before my eyes. As we were sitting at supper, I picked up the dishes and threw them into the yard. It was evening. We got up and went together to Sheik Mehdi and in his presence I divorced my wife three times.* He shook his head. The next day I was sorry, but what was the use, when being sorry wouldn't help and my wife was forbidden to me? For several days I prowled around the streets and the bazaar like a madman. I was so distracted that if an acquaintance ran into me, I couldn't return his greeting.

"I was never happy again after that. I couldn't forget her, even for a minute. I couldn't eat or sleep. I couldn't bear to be in the house: the walls cursed me. For two months I was ill in bed. All the time I was delirious I kept calling her name. When I began to recover, it was obvious that I could have had a hundred girls if I was interested. But she was something else. Finally I resolved that no matter what it took, I would marry her again. The time during which she couldn't remarry came to an end. I tried everything, but I saw it wasn't any use. I sold everything I had, even the junk: I got together eighteen tomans. There wasn't any other choice except to find a legalizer, someone who would marry my wife and then divorce her, so that after the one hundred day waiting period, I could remarry her.

"There was a clownish good-for-nothing grocer in our neighbourhood. Even if seven dogs licked his face, it wouldn't get clean. He was the kind who would cut off someone's head for an onion. I went and arranged it with him so that he would marry Robabeh, then divorce her, and I would pay all the expenses plus five tomans. And he accepted. One shouldn't be fooled by people – that bastard, that good-for-nothing..."

Shahbaz, pale, hid his face in his hands and said, "He was a grocer? What was his name? What kind of grocer was he? What neighbourhood was he from? No... No... Nothing like that could happen."

But Mirza Yadollah was so involved in what he was saying, and the past events had become so vivid to him, that he didn't stop.

"That damn grocer married my wife. You don't know how hard I took it. A woman who had been mine for three years. If someone had mentioned her name I would have torn him apart. Think of it: now, with my own help, she had to become the wife of that damned illiterate grocer. I said to myself, 'Maybe this is the revenge of my temporary wives, who cried when I divorced them.' Anyway, early the next morning I went to the grocer's house. He kept me waiting for an hour, which seemed a century to me. When he came I said to him, 'Stick to your bargain, divorce Robabeh, and you've made five tomans.' I can still picture his devilish face. He laughed and said, 'She's my wife, I wouldn't sell a hair on her head for a thousand tomans.' My eyes were blasting lightning!"

Shahbaz trembled and said, "No, something like that couldn't happen. Tell me the truth. God!…"

Mirza Yadollah said, "Now do you see that I was right? Now do you understand why I can't stand grocers? When he said he wouldn't give up a hair of her head for a thousand tomans, I understood that he wanted to get more money. But who had the time to bargain? I was hurting. I was horrified. I was so upset, and I was so sick and tired of life, that I didn't answer him. I gave him a look which was worse than any curse. From there I went directly to a second-hand store. I sold my robe and my cloak and bought a buckram robe. I put on a felt hat, adjusted my shoes, and set out. Since then I've been wandering from one town to the next, from one village to another, like a bewildered vagabond. It's been twelve years. I couldn't stay in one place any longer. Sometimes I work as a storyteller, sometimes as a teacher. I write letters for people, I recite the *Shahnameh* in teahouses, I play the flute. I enjoy seeing the world and its people. I want to spend my life just like this. One gets a lot out of it. In any case, we're old. We're flogging a dead horse. We've got one foot in this world and one in the next. It's too bad that we can't take advantage of the experience we've gained. How well the poet said it:

> A wise and skilful man
> Should live not once, but twice:
> At first to gain experience,
> Then to follow his own advice."

At this point Mirza Yadollah grew tired. It was as if his jaws stopped working because he had thought and spoken more than usual. He reached out and took his pipe, staring at the ricer and listening to the faint muffled melody which came from beyond the mountain.

Shahbaz raised his head from his hands. He sighed and said, "Every pair of actions requires a third to be complete!"

Mirza Yadollah was confused and didn't notice.

Shahbaz said louder, "She's sure to turn yet another wealthy man into a destitute tramp."

Yadollah came to himself and said, "Who?"

"That bitch Robabeh."

Mirza Yadollah's eyes popped out. Shocked, he asked, "What do you mean?"

Mashadi Shahbaz gave a forced laugh. "It's true that life really changes man. His face becomes wrinkled, his hair turns white, his teeth fall out. His voice changes. You didn't recognize me and I didn't recognize you."

Mirza Yadollah asked, "What?"

"Didn't Robabeh have a pockmark on her face? Didn't she blink a lot?"

Irritated, Mirza Yadollah said, "Who told you?"

Mashadi Shahbaz laughed, "Aren't you Sheikh Yadollah, the son of the late Sheikh Rasol, who lived in the alley with the public bath? You passed my store every morning. I am the legalizer, the same one."

Miraz Yadollah looked closer and said, "You're the one who has made this my life for the past twelve years? You are Shahbaz the grocer? There was a time when we would have fought it out if I had found you in these mountains. What a pity that time has tied the hands of both of us." Then he babbled to himself, "Very good, Robabeh, you've taken my revenge for me. He is wandering too, just like me." Once again he fell silent, his lips set in a painful smile.

The person sleeping on the bench opposite them rolled, sat up, yawned, and rubbed his eyes.

Mashadi Shahbaz and Mirza Yadollah glanced stealthily at each other, afraid to let their eyes meet. Two miserable enemies, with their struggles in love behind them. Now they should be thinking about death.

After a short silence, Shahbaz turned towards the coffeehouse patron and said, "Dash Akbar, bring us two cups of tea."

Whirlpool

(from *Three Drops of Blood*)

H OMAYOUN WAS WHISPERING to himself, "Is this real?... Could this be possible? So young but lying in the cold damp earth out there in the Shah Abdolazim cemetery* among thousands of other corpses... The shroud sticking to his body. Never again to see the arrival of spring or the end of autumn or suffocating sad days like today... Have the light of his eye and the song of his voice been completely turned off?... He who was so full of laughter and said such entertaining things?..."

The sky was overcast and the window was covered in a slim layer of steam. Looking out of the window you could see the neighbour's house. The neighbour's tin roof was covered with a thin coating of snow. Snowflakes were spinning slowly and neatly in the air before landing on the edge of the tin roof. Black smoke was coming out of the chimney, writhing and twisting in the grey sky and then disappearing slowly.

Homayoun was sitting in front of the gas heater together with his young wife and their little daughter, Homa. They were in the family room but unlike the past, when laughter and happiness ruled in this room on Fridays, today they all were sad and silent. Even their little daughter who usually livened things up looked dull and gloomy today. She had put a plaster-made doll next to her – the doll had a broken face – and was staring outside. It was as if she too was sensing that something was wrong, and the thing that was wrong was the fact that dear Uncle Bahram had failed to come to see them as was his habit. She was also feeling that her parents' sadness was on his account: the black clothes, the eyes red-rimmed from the lack of sleep, and the cigarette smoke which waved in the air all reinforced this suspicion.

Homayoun was staring at the fire in the gas heater, but his thoughts were elsewhere. Against his own will, his thoughts had wandered off

29

to his school days in winter. Days like today, when snow was one foot high. As soon as the bell rang to announce the break, no one had a chance against him and Bahram. They always played the same game. They would roll a ball of snow on the ground until it became a big pile. Then the children would split into two groups, and use the pile as a barricade, and so snowball fights would begin. Without feeling the cold, with red hands that burned with the intensity of the cold, they would throw snowballs at each other. One day when they were busy with this game, Homayoun pressed together a handful of icy snow and threw it at Bahram, cutting his forehead. The supervisor came and hit the palm of his hand with several sharp lashes. Perhaps it was then that his friendship with Bahram started, and until recently whenever he saw the scar on Bahram's forehead he would remember the beating on the palm of his hand. In the span of eighteen years their spirit and thought had come so close together that not only did they tell each other their very private thoughts and feelings, but they perceived many of each other's unspoken inner thoughts.

The two of them had almost exactly the same thoughts, the same taste, and were almost of the same disposition. Until now there had not arisen between them the least difference of opinion or the smallest offence. Then, on the morning of the day before yesterday, Homayoun had received a phone call in the office that Bahram Mirza had killed himself. That very hour Homayoun got a droshky and went hurriedly to Bahram's bedside. He slowly pulled back the white cloth that was covering Bahram's face – it was bloodstained. His eyelashes were covered in blood, his brain had splashed on the pillow, there were blood stains on the rug and the crying and distress of his relatives affected Homayoun as if he had been hit by a thunderbolt. Later, step by step, he walked alongside the coffin until near sunset when they buried him in the earth. He sent for a bouquet of flowers which was brought. He placed it on the grave and after the last goodbye he returned home with a heavy heart. But since that day he hadn't had a peaceful minute, he hadn't been able to sleep, and white hair had appeared on his temples. A packet of cigarettes was in front of him, and he smoked continuously.

It was the first time that Homayoun had thought deeply and reflected on the problem of death, but his thoughts led nowhere. No opinion or supposition could content him.

30

He was completely astonished and didn't know what to do. Sometimes a state of insanity would come over him. No matter how much he tried he couldn't forget. Their friendship had started in primary school and their lives had been almost entirely entwined. They were partners in sorrow and happiness, and every instant that he turned and looked at Bahram's picture all his past memories of Bahram would come alive and he would see him: the blond moustache, the blue, wide-set eyes, the small mouth, the narrow chin, his loud laugh and the way he cleared his throat were all before his eyes. He couldn't believe that Bahram was dead, and that he had died so suddenly!... What self-sacrifices hadn't Bahram made for him, in the three years that he had been away on duty and Bahram had been taking care of his household! According to Homayoun's wife, Badri, "He did everything for us. We didn't have to worry about a thing."

Now Homayoun felt the burden of life, and he missed the bygone days when they would gather so intimately in this same room. They would play backgammon and would completely lose track of time. But the thing that tortured him most was the thought that since they were so close together and hid nothing from each other, why hadn't Bahram consulted with him before deciding to commit suicide? What was the cause? Had he gone crazy or had there been a family secret involved? He would ask himself this question continually. At last it seemed that an idea had occurred to him. He sought refuge with his wife, Badri, and asked her, "Have you got any suspicion? Any idea why Bahram did this?"

Badri, who was seemingly preoccupied with embroidery, raised her head and, as if she had not expected this type of question, said unwillingly, "How am I supposed to know? Didn't he tell you?"

"No... That's why I asked... I'm surprised by that too... When I came back from the trip I felt that he had changed. But he didn't say anything to me. I thought this preoccupation of his was because of his office work... Because being cooped up made him depressed, he had told me many times... But he didn't hide anything from me."

"God bless him! How lively and happy he was. This is unlike him."

"No, he pretended to be like that; sometimes he would change and be very different... When he was alone... Once when I entered his room and didn't recognize him, he had put his head between his hands and he was thinking. As soon as he saw that I was startled he laughed and made the usual jokes in order to cover up. He was a good actor!"

"Maybe there was something that he was afraid of telling you for fear of hurting you. He was probably being considerate and was thinking of you. After all, you have a wife and a child, so you have to think about getting on in life. But he…" She shook her head in a meaningful way, as if his suicide had no importance. Once more the silence obliged them to think. Homayoun felt that his wife's words were not sincere and she had said them for the sake of expediency. The same woman who eight years ago used to worship him, who had such delicate thoughts about love! He felt as if a curtain had lifted from before his eyes. His wife's attempt at consoling him had made him feel disgusted with her, especially in the face of his memories of Bahram. He became weary of his wife. She had become materialistic, wise and mature, and had started to think of wealth and worldly life and didn't want to give way to sadness and sorrow. And the reason she gave was that Bahram didn't have a wife and child. What a mean thought. Since he had deprived himself of this common pleasure, his death held no cause for regret. Was his child worth more in the world than his friend? Never! Wasn't Bahram worthy of regret? Would he find anyone else like him in the world?

That Bahram should die and this mumbling ninety-year-old, Sayyed Khanom, should live! She had come today, in the snow and cold, hobbling with a walking stick all the way from Pah Chenar,* looking for Bahram's house to eat the halva given out to invoke God's blessing. This was God's policy, and in his wife's opinion it was natural, and his wife Badri too would someday come to look like this Sayyed Khanom. Even now that she is not wearing make-up she looks different. Her appearance had changed a lot. Her voice and the expression of her eyes had changed. In the early morning when he went to work she would still be asleep. There were crow's feet around her eyes and they had lost their lustre. Probably his wife had the same feeling about him too, who knew? Hadn't he himself changed? Was he the same old kind, obedient and good looking Homayoun? Hadn't he cheated on his wife? But why had this thought occurred to him? Was it because of the lack of sleep or the painful reminiscence about his friend?

At this point the door opened and a servant, who held the corner of her *chador* between her teeth, brought a large sealed letter, gave it to Homayoun, and left. Homayoun recognized Bahram's short, irregular handwriting on the envelope, opened it with haste, pulled out a letter and read:

Now, at 1:30 in the morning on the thirteenth day of Mehr 1311,* *I, Bahram Mirza Arjanpour, of my own free will and preference am bequeathing all my possessions to Miss Homa Mahafarid.*

Bahram Arjanpour

Astonished, Homayoun reread the letter and then, in a state of amazement, let it slip through his hand.

Badri, who was watching him out of the corner of her eye, asked, "Who is the letter from?"

"Bahram."

"What does he say?"

"Do you know that he has given all his possessions to Homa?"

"What a fine man!"

This expression of surprise mixed with affability made Bahram even more disgusted with his wife. But involuntarily his glance caught Bahram's picture. Then he looked back at Homa. Suddenly something occurred to him so that he started to tremble helplessly. It was as if another curtain had fallen before his eyes: there was no doubt that his daughter resembled Bahram. She didn't look like him or her mother. Neither one of them had blue eyes. The small mouth, the narrow chin, in fact all the features on her face were just like those of Bahram. Homayoun came to understand why Bahram had loved Homa so dearly and why after his death he had bequeathed her all his possessions! Was this child whom he loved so much the result of intimacy between Bahram and his wife? And Bahram, a friend whose soul was in the same mould as his and in whom he had so much trust? His wife had been intimate with him for years without his knowing it and Bahram had deceived him all this time, had mocked him and now he had sent this will too, this insult after death. No, he couldn't tolerate all this. These thoughts passed like lightning through his mind. His head ached, his cheeks felt cold, he turned a fiery gaze on Badri and said, "What do you say, huh, why did Bahram do this? Didn't he have sisters and brothers?"

"Because he loved this child. When you were at Bandargaz,* Homa got the measles. For ten days and nights that man was a nurse at the foot of this child's bed. God bless him!"

Homayoun said angrily, "No, it isn't that simple…"

"Why isn't it that simple? Not everyone is indifferent like you are, going away and leaving your wife and child for three years. And when you returned, you came back empty handed; you didn't even bring me a pair of stockings. People show affection through giving. To him, loving your child was the same as loving you. After all, he was not in love with Homa! And then didn't you realize that she was the apple of his eye?…"

"No, you aren't telling me the truth."

"What do you want me to say? I don't understand."

"You're feigning ignorance."

"Meaning what?… Someone else kills himself, someone else gives away his belongings and I am being held to account?"

"That much I know for sure: you're not telling everything."

"You know what? I don't understand hints and allusions. Go and get medical treatment, you're not feeling well, your mind is all over the place. What do you want from me?"

"Do you believe that I don't know?"

"If you know then why do you ask me?"

Homayoun shouted with impatience, "Enough is enough. You're mocking me!" Then he picked up Bahram's will, crumpled it and threw it in the gas heater where it flared up and turned to ashes.

Badri flung down the purple cloth she had in her hand, got up, and said, "So you're being spiteful to me, that's fine, but why can't you allow your own child some indulgence?" Homayoun got up, leant against the table and in an ironic tone said, "My child… my child?… Then why does she look like Bahram?" With his elbow he hit the inlaid frame which held Bahram's picture and it fell to the floor.

The child, who had been sulking till now, burst into a loud crying. Badri, looking pale, said in a threatening tone, "What do you mean? What are you intending to say?"

"I want to say that you have fooled me for eight years, mocked me. For eight years you've been a disgrace to me, not a wife…"

"To me?… To my daughter?"

Homayoun showed the picture with an angry laugh and said, breathing heavily, "Yes, your daughter... your daughter... Pick her up and have a look at her. I want to say that now my eyes are opened, I understand why he left everything to her, he was a kind father. But you – it's been eight years that..."

"That I've been in your house, that I've suffered every kind of hardship, that I put up with your misfortunes, that I took care of your household for three years when you weren't here, then, later I found out that you had fallen in love with a Russian slut in Bandargaz, and now I get this reward. You can't find any excuse so you say my child looks like Bahram. But I can no longer put up with this. I won't stay in this house for another minute. Come darling... let's go."

Homa, pale and in a state of fright, was trembling and watching this strange and unprecedented quarrel between her father and her mother. Crying, she took hold of her mother's skirt and the two of them went towards the door. Near the door Badri took a key chain from her pocket and threw it heavily so that it rolled in front of Homayoun's feet. The sounds of Homa's crying and of footsteps in the hall became faint. Ten minutes later the sound of the wheels of a droshky was heard carrying them off in the snow and cold. Homayoun stood astonished and giddy in his place. He was afraid to lift his head: he didn't want to believe that these events were real. He was asking himself if he had gone crazy or was having a nightmare. At any rate, the thing that was evident was that this house and this life had become unbearable for him, and his daughter Homa, whom he loved so much, he couldn't see any more. He couldn't kiss her and caress her. The memories of his friend had become stained. Worse than everything else was that, unbeknown to him, for eight years his wife had been cheating on him with his only friend and had polluted the heart of his family. All of this hidden from him, without his knowing it! They had all been very good actors. He was the only one who had been fooled, and ridiculed. Suddenly he became completely weary of his life, he was disillusioned with everything and everyone. He felt limitlessly alone and alienated. He had no other choice but to be sent on a bureaucratic mission to a distant city or to a port in the south and pass the rest of his life there, or else do away with himself: go somewhere he wouldn't see anyone, wouldn't hear anyone's voice, sleep in a ditch and never wake again. Because for the first time he felt that between him and all the people who were around him a frightening whirlpool existed that he hadn't perceived until now.

He lit a cigarette and took several paces. Once again he leant against the table. Outside the window snowflakes were landing on the edge of the tin roof neatly, slowly, and heedlessly, as if they were dancing to the tune of mysterious music. Without intending to, he remembered the happy and wholesome days when he and his father and mother would go to their village in Iraq. During the days he would sleep by himself on the grass under the shade of the trees, the same place where Shir Ali would smoke his pipe and sit on the wheel of the threshing machine. Shir Ali's daughter, who had a red *chador*, would spend long hours there waiting for her father. The threshing machine with its plaintive sound would crush the golden stalks of wheat. The cows with long horns and wide foreheads whose necks had been scarred by the yoke walked in circles until nightfall. Now his condition was like that of those cows. Now he knew what these animals had been feeling. He too had passed his life with closed eyes, in an endless circle, like a horse on a treadmill, like those cows that crushed the stalks of wheat. He remembered the monotonous hours when he sat behind a desk in the small customs room and continually scribbled out the same papers. Sometimes his colleague would look at his watch and yawn, but he would carry on, writing the same numbers in their proper columns. He would check, add, turn the notebooks inside out – but at that time he had something to be happy about. He knew that although his vision, his thought, his youth, and his strength were diminishing bit by bit, he still had something to keep him happy. He knew that when he returned home at night and saw Bahram, his daughter and his wife smiling, his tiredness would disappear. But now he was disgusted with all three of them. It was the three of them who had brought him to such a pass.

As if he had made a sudden decision, he went to his desk and sat down. He pulled out a drawer and took out a small pistol that he always carried when he was travelling. He checked it. The bullets were in their place. He looked inside the cold black barrel and moved the pistol slowly towards his temple, but then remembered Bahram's bloody face. Finally he put it away in the pocket of his trousers.

He got up again. In the hall he put on his overcoat and galoshes. He picked up the umbrella too and left the house. The alley was empty. Snowflakes were whirling slowly in the air. He set out without hesitation, although he didn't know where he was going. He just wanted to flee, to get far away from his house, from these frightening events.

He came out on a street which was cold, white and sad. Passing droshky wheels had formed furrows in the middle of the street. He was walking with long footsteps. An automobile passed him, and watery snow and mud from the street spattered on his head and face. He stood and looked at his clothes. They had been drenched in mud and it was as if they gave him consolation. As he went he came across a little boy selling matches. He called him. He bought a box of matches, but when he looked at the boy's face he saw he had blue eyes, small lips and blond hair. He remembered Bahram, his body trembled, and he continued on his way. Suddenly he stopped before the window of a shop. He went forwards and pressed his forehead against the cold glass. His hat almost fell off. Toys were arranged behind the window. He rubbed his sleeve on the glass to clean off the steam but it was useless. A big doll with a red face and blue eyes stood in front of him smiling. He stared at it for a while. He thought of how happy Homa would be if this doll belonged to her. The store owner opened the door. He started out again, and passed two more alleys. On his path a poultry seller was sitting next to his basket. Inside the basket, there had been put three hens and a rooster whose legs were tied together. Their red legs trembled from the cold. Red drops of blood had fallen near the poultry seller on the snow. A little further on, sitting in front of a house, was a boy with ringworm. The boy's arms stuck out of a torn shirt.

He noticed all this without recognizing his surroundings or route. He didn't feel the falling snow, and the closed umbrella he had picked up he held shut in his hand. He went into another empty alley and sat on the front steps of a house. The snow was falling faster. He opened his umbrella. A deep weariness had taken possession of him. His head felt heavy. His eyes slowly closed. The sound of passing voices brought him to himself. He got up. The sky had become dark. He remembered all the day's events: the boy with ringworm that he had seen in front of a house and whose arms were visible from under his torn shirt, the red, wet legs of the hens in the basket that were trembling from the cold, and the blood which had fallen on the snow. He felt a little hungry. He bought sweet bread from a bakery. He ate it as he walked and, without intending to, prowled around the alley like a shadow.

When he entered his house, it was two in the morning. He fell into the armchair. An hour later he woke up from the force of the cold, lay down on the bed in his clothes, and pulled the quilt over his head. He dreamt that in a room somewhere the same boy who was selling matches was dressed in black and was seated behind a desk on which was a big doll with blue smiling eyes, and in front of him three people were standing with their hands folded on their chests. His daughter Homa entered. She had a candle in her hand. After her a man entered who was wearing a white and bloodstained mask on his face. The man moved forwards and took the hands of Homa and the boy. Just as Homayoun wanted to go out of the door two hands came out from behind the curtain, holding pistols in his direction. Frightened, Homayoun jumped awake with a headache.

For two weeks his life passed in the same way. During the days he went to his office and only returned very late at night to sleep. Sometimes in the afternoons for no reason that he could think of he would pass near the girls' school that Homa attended. After school he would hide at the corner behind the wall, fearing he would be seen by Mashdi Ali, his father-in-law's servant. He looked the children over one by one, but he didn't see his daughter Homa among them, and life carried on in this manner until his request for a transfer was accepted and he was directed to go to the customs office in Kermanshah.

The day before leaving Homayoun made all his preparations. He even went to see that the bus was in the garage and bought the ticket. Since his suitcases were not packed he arranged to leave for Kermanshah the next morning, instead of going that very afternoon, as the garage owner had insisted.

When he entered his house he immediately went to the family room where his desk was. The room was disorganized and messy. Cold ashes had fallen in front of the gas heater. The piece of embroidered purple silk and the envelope of Bahram's will had been put on the table. He picked up the envelope and tore it down the middle, but then he saw a piece of written paper he hadn't noticed that day in his great haste. After he had put the pieces together on the table he read:

Probably this letter will come to you after my death. I know you will be surprised at this sudden decision of mine, since I did nothing without your advice, but so that there won't be any mystery between us I confess that I loved your wife Badri. I fought with myself for four years. At last I won, and I killed the demon that had awakened in me, so that I might not betray you. I give a worthless present to Homa that I hope will be accepted!

    Yours always,

            Bahram

For a while Homayoun stared around the room astonished. He no longer doubted that Homa was his own child. Could he have left without seeing Homa? He read the letter again and a third time. He put it in his pocket and left the house. On his way he entered the toy shop and without hesitation bought the big doll with the red face and blue eyes and went towards his father-in-law's house. When he got there he knocked on the door. When he saw Homayoun, Mashdi Ali the servant said with eyes full of tears, "Sir, what calamity has happened? Miss Homa!"

"What's happened?"

"Sir, you don't know how restless Miss Homa was at being away from you. I would take her to school every day. It was Sunday. Up to now that makes five days since the afternoon that she ran away from school. She had said she was going to see her dear father. We were in a frenzy. But didn't Muhammad tell you? We telephoned the police, I came to your house twice."

"What are you saying? What has happened?"

"Nothing, sir, it was evening when they brought her home. She had got lost. She got pneumonia from the terrible cold. She called you continually until the moment she died. Yesterday we took her to Shah Abdolazim. We buried her right next to Bahram Mirza's grave."

Homayoun was staring at Mashdi Ali. At this point the doll box fell from his arms. Then like a crazed man he pulled up the collar of his overcoat and went towards the garage with long strides, because he had changed his mind about packing the suitcases, and he could leave much sooner on the afternoon bus.

Fire-Worshipper

(from *Buried Alive*)

F LANDON,* who had just returned from Iran, was sitting opposite one of his old friends in a room on the third floor of a Parisian guesthouse. A bottle of wine and two glasses were put on a small table between the friends and music was playing in the café below. Outside it was dark and cloudy and a light rain was falling. Flandon lifted his head from his hands, picked up a glass of wine, drained it and turned to his friend. "Do you know – there was a time when I felt that I had lost myself among those ruins, mountains, and deserts. I said to myself, 'Could it be that one day I'll return to my country? Would I be able to hear this same music that is playing now?' I wished to return some day. I wished for an hour like this when we could be alone and I could open my heart to you. But now I want to tell you something different, something that I know you won't believe: now that I've come back, I regret it. You know, I still long for Iran. It's as if I've lost something!"

On hearing this, his friend, whose face had turned red and whose eyes were wide but expressionless, jokingly hit the table with his fist and laughed out loud. "Eugene stop joking. I know you were a painter, but I didn't know you were also a poet. So you've become tired of us? Tell me, you must have become attached to someone down there. I've heard that Eastern women are pretty."

"No, it's nothing like that. I'm not joking."

"By the way, the other day I was with your brother and the conversation turned to you. He brought several recent pictures which you had sent from Iran and we looked at them. I remember they were all pictures of ruins... Oh yes, he said one of them was a place for worshipping fire. You mean they worship fire there? The only thing I know about the country you were in is that they have good carpets: I don't know anything else. Now you describe to me everything that you've seen. You know, everything about it is new for us Parisians."

41

Flandon was silent a moment, then said, "You've reminded me of something. One day in Iran something took place which was very strange for me. Up to now I haven't told anyone, not even my friend Coste, who was with me. I was afraid he would laugh at me. You know that I don't believe in anything. Only once in all my life have I worshipped God sincerely, with all my heart and soul. That was in Iran, near the same fire temple you saw the picture of. One night, when I was in the south of Iran excavating at Persepolis, I had gone alone to Nagshe Rostam. There the graves of ancient Persian kings were carved into the mountain. I think you may have seen the picture. It's something like a cross that has been carved into the mountain. Above it is a picture of the king standing in front of the fire temple with his right arm raised towards the fire. Above the fire temple is Ahura Mazda, their god. Below the temple the stone has been cut in the form of a porch, and the king's tomb is located within the stone crypt. Several of those crypts can be seen there. Opposite them is the great fire temple, which is called the Kaaba of Zoroaster.

"Anyway, I remember clearly that it was near dusk. I was busy measuring this same temple. I was almost worn out with fatigue and the heat. Suddenly I saw two people, whose clothes were different from ordinary Persian clothes, coming towards me. When they got closer, I saw that they were two old men. Two old but strong, lively men with sparkling eyes and striking faces. I asked them questions and it became evident that they were merchants from Yazd who had come from the north of Iran. Their religion was like that of most of the inhabitants of Yazd. In other words, they were fire-worshippers like the ancient kings of Iran. They had deliberately gone out of their way to make a pilgrimage to the ancient fire temple. They hadn't finished talking when they began to gather pieces of wood and twigs and dry leaves. They piled them up and made a small fire. I stood still, astonished, and watched them. They lit the dry wood and started to say prayers and murmur in a special language which I had not heard before. Probably it was the language of Zoroaster and the Avesta; maybe it was the same language which had been carved in cuneiform on the rocks.

"At this point, when the two fire-worshippers were busy praying in front of the fire, I lifted my head. I saw that the scene carved in the stone exactly resembled the living scene in front of me. I stood frozen in my tracks. It was as if these people on the stone exactly above the grave of Darius had come to life and after several thousand years had come down opposite me to worship the manifestation of their god: I was amazed that after this length of time, in spite of the effort expended by the Muslims to destroy and overthrow this faith, this ancient religion still had followers who, secretly but in the open air, threw themselves to the ground before the fire!

"The two fire-worshippers left and disappeared. I remained alone, but the small fire was still burning. I don't know how it happened – but I felt that I was under pressure by a religious force and tension. A heavy silence ruled there. The moon had come out from the side of the mountain like a fiery sphere of sulphur and its pale light had illuminated the body of the great fire temple. Time seemed to have gone backwards two or three thousand years. I had forgotten my nationality, personality, and surroundings. I looked at the ashes in front of which those two mysterious old men had fallen down in worship and praise. Blue smoke was slowly rising from the spot in the shape of a column and was spiralling in the air. The shadow of broken stones, the blurred horizon, the stars which shone above my head and winked to each other, the display of the quiet and splendour of the plain among these mysterious ruins and ancient fire temples – it was as if the surroundings, the souls of all the dead, and the power of their thought, which was aloft over the crypt and the broken stones, had forced or inspired me, because things were no longer in my hands. I, who had no belief in anything, fell involuntarily to my knees before these ashes from which the blue smoke rose, and worshipped them: I didn't know what to say but I didn't need to murmur anything. Perhaps less than a minute passed before I came to myself again, but I worshiped the manifestation of Ahura Mazda – perhaps in the same way the ancient kings of Iran worshipped fire. In that moment I was a fire-worshipper. Now, think whatever you like about me. Maybe it was just because mankind is weak and is not capable…"

Abji Khanom

(from *Buried Alive*)

Abji khanom was marokh's older sister, but anyone who didn't know the family would have found it hard to believe that they were sisters. Abji Khanom was tall, lanky, swarthy with thick lips and coarse black hair. She was altogether ugly. Marokh, on the other hand, was petite, fair, with a small nose and chestnut hair. Her eyes were alluring, and every time she laughed dimples appeared. They were very different from each other with regard to behaviour and habit too. Ever since she was a child, Abji Khanom had been fussy and quarrelsome and didn't get along with people. She would even sulk at her mother for two or three months at a time. Her sister, by contrast, was tactful and appealing. She was always good natured and laughing. Naneh Hasan, their neighbour, had nicknamed her "Miss Favourite". Even her mother and father loved Marokh more, since she was the youngest child and their dear darling.

Abji Khanom's mother used to hit her when she was a child. She would nag her and make a fuss but publicly, in front of the neighbours and other people, she would pretend that she felt sorry for Abji Khanom. She would cross her hands and say, "What can I do with this bad luck, eh? Who will marry such an ugly girl? I am afraid she will remain at home. A girl who has no wealth, no beauty, and no accomplishment. Who is the miserable person who will marry her?" Words like this had been repeated in the presence of Abji Khanom so many times that she too had totally lost hope, and had given up on the idea of finding a husband. She spent most of her time praying and fulfilling religious duties. She had completely given up on marriage, since no husband had appeared for her. Once they wanted to give her to Kalb Hosein, the apprentice carpenter, but he didn't want her. Nonetheless, every time Abji Khanom met people, she would tell them, "I had a proposal but I turned it down. Today's husbands are all immoral drunkards, better dead than alive. I shall never get married."

She spoke like this on the surface, but it was evident that in her heart she liked Kalb Hosein and was very eager to get married. But since from the age of five she had been told that she was ugly and no one would marry her, and since she knew she had no share in the pleasures of this world, she wanted at least to receive the wealth of the other world by the power of prayer and worship. In this way she had found comfort for herself. Yes, why should she regret that she had no share in the pleasures of this transitory world? After all, the eternal world, the hereafter, would be all hers. Then all the attractive people, including her sister and everybody else, would wish they were her. When the months of Muharri and Safar* arrived, this was Abji Khanom's time to show off. There was no preaching at which she was not at the head of the crowd. In the passion plays* she would take a place for herself an hour before noon. All the preachers knew her and were very eager that Abji Khanom should be at the foot of their pulpits so that the crowd would get worked up from her crying groans and screams. She had memorized most of the sermons. She had heard the sermons so many times and she knew so many religious problems that most of the neighbours would come to her and ask about their mistakes. Early in the morning, she was the one in charge of waking up the household. First she would go to her sister's bed and kick her, saying, "It's almost noon. When are you going to get up and say your prayers?" The poor girl would get up, sleepily wash and stand up to say her prayers. The morning call to prayer, the cry of the rooster, the dawn breeze, the murmur of prayers, gave Abji Khanom a special feeling, a spiritual feeling, and she felt proud before her conscience. She would say to herself, "If God doesn't take me to heaven then whom will He take?" The rest of the day also, after doing some insignificant housework and fussing about this and that, she would take in her hand a long rosary, whose black colour had turned yellow from being handled so much, and recite the beads. Now her only wish was that, by whatever means, she could go on a pilgrimage trip to Karbala and stay there.

But her sister didn't show any special religious zeal and did all of the housework. Then when she was fifteen she went to work as a maid. Abji Khanom was twenty-two, but she was stuck at home and secretly envied her sister. During the year and a half that Marokh went away to work as a maid, not even once had Abji Khanom tried to visit her or asked how she was. When Marokh came home every two weeks to see her family, Abji Khanom would either quarrel with someone or go and pray, stretching it out for two or three hours. Also, later when everyone was sitting together, she would make sarcastic remarks to her sister and would begin lecturing her about prayers, fasting, cleanliness and scepticism. For example, she would say, "From the time when these modern, mincing women appeared, bread became more expensive... Whoever doesn't cover her face will be suspended by the hair in hell. Whoever talks behind someone's back will have her head as big as a mountain and her neck as thin as a hair. In hell there are such snakes that people take shelter with dragons." And she would go on in this vein. Marokh had felt that her sister was jealous but she pretended that she didn't notice.

One day towards evening, Marokh came home and talked quietly with her mother for a while and then left. Abji Khanom had gone to the entrance of the opposite room and had sat, puffing on a water pipe, but because of her jealousy she didn't ask her mother what her sister's conversation had been about and her mother said nothing about it either. In the evening when her father, with his egg-shaped hat on which whitewash had dried, came home from bricklaying, he changed his clothes, took his tobacco pouch and his pipe, and went up on the roof. Abji Khanom, leaving her work as it was, went with her mother and took the samovar, a pot, a copper container, and relish and onions. They sat next to each other on a carpet. Her mother started the conversation, saying that Abbas, a servant in the same house where Marokh worked, had proposed to her. This morning when the house was empty Abbas's mother had come to ask for her hand. They wanted to sign the marriage contract next week. They would give twenty-five tomans as a gift for the bride's mother, thirty tomans to the bride in case there was a divorce, as well as a mirror, candlesticks, a Koran, a pair of shoes, sweets, a bag of henna, a taffeta scarf, brocaded chintz trousers... Her father, fanning himself with a fan hemmed around the edges, sucking a piece of sugar in the corner of his mouth and drinking tea, nodded and said offhandedly, "Good enough. Congratulations. There's no objection." He didn't show any surprise or happiness and didn't express any opinion. It was as if he was afraid of his wife. But Abji Khanom was furious as soon as she heard this news. She couldn't listen to the rest of the agreements and on the pretext of prayers she got up without intending to and went downstairs to the main room which had five entrances. She stared at herself in a small mirror she had. In her own eyes she appeared old and broken down, as if these few minutes had aged her several years. She examined the wrinkle between her eyebrows. She found one white hair. With two fingers she pulled it out. She stared at it for a while under the light. Where she pulled it from she felt nothing.

Several days passed. There was quite a commotion at home. They went back and forth to the bazaar and bought two silk outfits, a water pitcher, glasses, embroidery, a rose water sprinkler, a drinking container, a night cap, a box of cosmetics, eyebrow paint, a bronze samovar, painted curtains, everything imaginable. Since the mother wanted a great deal for her daughter, whatever trinkets from the home came into her hands she would put aside for Marokh's trousseau. Even the hand-woven prayer carpets that Abji Khanom had asked her mother for several times and which she hadn't given to her she put aside for Marokh. During these several days Abji Khanom silently and apprehensively watched these things, pretending not to notice. For two days she pretended to have a headache and rested. Her mother repeatedly scorned her, saying, "When is sisterhood valuable, if not now? I know it's from jealousy, and no one reaches his goal from that. Besides, ugliness and beauty aren't in my hands, it's God's work. You saw that I wanted to give you to Kalb Hosein, but they didn't like you. Now you're pretending to be sick so you won't have to do anything. From morning till night you pretend to be pious, while I must strain my weak eyes sewing."

Furious with the jealousy which had overflowed her heart, Abji Khanom answered from under the quilt, "Enough, enough. She tries to put a brand in a heart of ice. Such a bridegroom you found her! Whenever you hit a dog someone like Abbas will appear in this town. What kind of taunt are you giving me? It's clear that everyone knows what kind of a man Abbas is. Now don't make me spell out that Marokh is two months pregnant. I saw that her stomach has swollen, but I didn't show that I noticed it. I no longer consider her my sister."

Her mother became very angry. "May God strike you dumb. Go and die. I hope you die, shameless girl. Go and get lost. Do you want to stain my daughter's reputation? I know this is just jealousy. You are dying because nobody will marry you with that face and figure. Now out of grief you slander your own sister. Didn't you say that God in his own Koran has written that a liar is a big sinner, eh? God had mercy on others that he did not make you pretty... Every other hour you leave the house on the pretext of going to a sermon. You're the one who makes people gossip... Go, go. All this praying and fasting isn't worth the curse of Satan for people who have been deceitful. You're just fooling people."

This kind of talk passed between them for the next several days. Marokh stared at these scuffles astonished and said nothing, until the night of the ceremony arrived. All the neighbours and the local unladylike women had gathered together, their eyes and eyebrows painted black, their faces white and their cheeks red. The women wore print *chadors*, had straight fringes and sported baggy cotton trousers. Among them Naneh Hasan was in the limelight. Simpering and smiling, she had tilted her head and was playing the drum. She sang whatever came to her mind:

> Oh friends, congratulations. With the blessing of God, congratulations.
> We came, we came again, we came from the bridegroom's home –
> Everybody's pretty as the moon, everybody's a king, everybody's got almond eyes.
> Oh friends, congratulations. With the blessing of God, congratulations.
> We came, we came again, we came from the bride's home.
> Everybody's blind, everybody's lethargic, everybody's with sick eyes.
> Oh friends, congratulations. We have come to take the angel and the fairy.
> With the blessing of God, congratulations.

She would repeat this same thing over and over. They came and went, cleaning trays by the fountain, rubbing them with ashes. The smell of vegetable stew permeated the air. Someone shooed a cat out of the kitchen. Someone wanted eggs for an omelette. Several small children had taken each other's hands and were sitting down and getting up saying, "The small bath has ants; sit down and get up." They lit bronze fires in rented samovars. Unexpectedly they had news that the lady of the house where Marokh was a maid was coming to the ceremony with her daughters. On two tables sweets and fruit were arranged and they put two chairs at each table. Marokh's father was pacing pensively, thinking that his expenditure had been great. But Marokh's mother was insisting that for the approaching night they should have a puppet show. In all this tumult there was no sign of Abji Khanom. She had been gone since two in the afternoon. No one knew where she was. Probably she had gone to listen to a sermon.

When the candles were lit and the ceremony was over, everyone had gone except for Naneh Hasan. They had joined the hands of the bride and groom who were sitting beside each other in the main room. The doors were closed. Abji Khanom entered the house. She went directly to the room next to the main room to take off her *chador*. As soon as she entered she noticed that they had pulled down the curtain in the main room. Out of curiosity she lifted a corner of the curtain from behind the glass. Under the light of the lamp, she saw her sister Marokh, looking prettier than ever with make-up and painted eyebrows, beside the bridegroom, who seemed to be about twenty. They were sitting in front of a table filled with sweets. The bridegroom put his hand around Marokh's waist and said something in her ear. It looked as if they had noticed Abji Khanom or maybe her sister had recognized her. To spite Abji Khanom, they laughed and then kissed. From the end of the courtyard came the sound of Naneh Hasan's drum. She was singing, "Oh friends, congratulations…" A feeling of hatred mixed with jealousy overcame Abji Khanom. She dropped the curtain and went and sat on the pile of bedding which they had put near the wall. Without opening her black *chador* she rested her chin in her hands and stared at the ground at the flower patterns of the carpet. She counted them and they seemed to her to be something new; she noticed the pattern of their colours. She either didn't notice anyone coming and going, or she wouldn't lift her head to see who it was. Her mother came to the door of her room and said to her, "Why don't you eat supper? Why do you make yourself suffer? Why are you sitting here? Take off your black *chador*. Why have you left it on like a bad omen? Come and kiss your sister. Come and watch them from behind the glass. The bride and groom look like the full moon. Aren't you happy for them? Come on, say something, finally. Everyone was asking where her sister was. I didn't know what to say."

Abji Khanom only raised her head and said, "I've eaten supper."

* * *

50

It was midnight. Everyone was asleep with the memory of his own wedding night and dreaming happy dreams. Suddenly, as if somebody were thrashing in water, the sound of splashing woke everybody abruptly. At first they thought a cat or a child had fallen into the fountain. With bare heads and feet they lit the lights. They searched everywhere but found nothing extraordinary. When they came back to go to sleep Naneh Hasan saw that Abji Khanom's slippers had fallen near the cover of the water reservoir. They brought the light forwards and saw Abji Khanom's body floating on the water surface. Her braided black hair had wrapped around her throat like a snake. Her rust-coloured clothes clung to her body. Her face shone with splendour and luminosity. It was as if she had gone to a place where there existed neither ugliness nor beauty, neither marriage nor funerals, neither laughter nor crying, neither happiness nor sorrow. She had gone to heaven.

The Stray Dog

(from *The Stray Dog*)

VARAMIN SQUARE WAS MADE UP of several small shops – a bakery, a butcher's shop, a chemist, two cafés and a hairdresser's, all of which served to fulfil the most basic needs of life. Beneath the powerful sun the square and its residents were half burnt, half broiled. They longed for the first evening breeze and the shade of the night. The people, the shops, the train and the animals had ceased their activity. The warm weather weighed heavily on them and a fine mist of dust, continually increased by the coming and going of cars, shimmered under the azure sky.

On one side of the square was an old sycamore tree whose trunk was hollow and rotten but whose crooked, rheumatic branches had spread out with a desperate stubbornness. In the shade of its dusty leaves a large, wide bench had been placed from which two little boys with loud voices were selling rice pudding and pumpkin seeds. Thick muddy water pushed itself with difficulty through the ditch in front of the café.

The only building which attracted attention was the well-known tower of Varamin, half of whose cracked, cylindrical body and cone-shaped top was visible. Even the sparrows that had built nests in the crevice where bricks had fallen from the tower were quiet from the force of the heat and were having a nap. The moaning of a dog was the only sound to break the stillness at intervals.

The dog was from Scotland and had a smoky grey snout and black spots on his legs, looking as if he had run through a marsh and been splashed with slime. He had drooping ears, a bristling tail, and matt, dirty fur. Two human eyes shone in his woolly face. A human spirit could be seen in the depths of his eyes. Even in the darkness which had overtaken his life, there was in his eyes something eternal and shining, something which held a message that couldn't be understood. It was neither brightness nor colour: it was something indefinable. Not only did there exist a similarity between his eyes and human eyes, but also a kind of equality could be seen. Two hazel eyes full of pain, torment and hope, eyes that can only be seen in the face of a wandering dog. But it seemed as if no one saw or understood his pained, pleading looks. In front of the bakery the errand boy would hit him. In front of the butcher's the apprentice would throw stones at him. If he took shelter in the shade of a car, a heavy kick from the driver's shoe would greet him. And when everyone else grew tired of tormenting him, the boy who sold rice pudding took special pleasure in torturing him. For every groan the dog gave, he would be hit in the side with a stone. The sound of the boy's loud laughter would rise above the moans of the dog, and he would say, "God damn." It was as if all the others were on the boy's side, craftily and slyly encouraging him and then doubling up with laughter. They all hit the dog for God's sake, since in their opinion it was quite natural that they should hurt the unclean dog which their religion had cursed and which they believed had seventy lives.

Eventually, the rice pudding boy's torment forced the animal to flee down the alley which led towards the tower. He didn't really flee, he dragged himself with difficulty, on an empty stomach, and took shelter in a water channel. He laid his head on his paws, let his tongue hang out and, half asleep, half awake, looked at the green field which waved before him. His body was exhausted and his nerves were overwrought.

In the moist air of the water channel a special tranquillity enveloped him from head to foot. In his nostrils the different odours of half-dead weeds, an old damp shoe, the smell of live and dead animals brought to life half-suppressed memories.

Whenever he looked carefully at the green field, his instinctive desires would awaken, and memories of the past would be brought to his mind afresh, but this time the sensation was so powerful that it felt as if a voice he could hear next to his ear was compelling him to move about, jump and leap. He felt an inordinate desire to run and frolic in the green fields.

This was his inherited feeling: all his ancestors had been bred among the green open fields of Scotland. But his body was so exhausted that it didn't allow him to make the slightest movement. A painful feeling mixed with weakness overcame him. A handful of forgotten feelings, lost feelings had reawakened. Once, he had had various duties and responsibilities. He knew himself bound to answer his master's call, to drive out strange people and dogs from his master's home, to play with his master's child, to act one way with acquaintances and another with strangers, to eat on time, to expect being fondled at a certain time. But now all these ties had been removed.

All of his attention had narrowed down to finding a bit of food, fearfully and tremblingly, in the rubbish heap, while taking blows and howling all day – this had become his only means of defence. Formerly he had been courageous, fearless, clean, and full of life, but now he had become timid, the butt of people's vengeance. Whatever noise he heard or whatever moved near him caused him to tremble. He was even frightened of his own voice. He had become accustomed to rubbish. His body itched, but he didn't have the heart to search for fleas or to lick himself clean. He felt he had become part of the garbage, and something in him had died, had gone out.

Two winters had passed since he had found himself in this hell. During this time he hadn't eaten a full meal, or taken a peaceful nap. His lustre and passions had been stifled. Not a single person had laid a caressing hand on his head. Not one resembled his master in appearance – it seemed that in feelings, disposition and behaviour, his owner was a world away from these people. It was as if the people he had formerly been with were closer to his world, understood his pain and his feelings better, and protected him.

From among the smells which assailed his nostrils, the one that dizzied him the most was the smell of that boy's rice pudding: that white liquid which was so similar to his mother's milk and which brought to mind the memories of his childhood. Suddenly a numbness took hold of him. He remembered as a puppy sucking that warm, nutritious liquid from his mother's breast while her warm, firm tongue licked his body clean. The strong odour he had breathed in his mother's embrace, next to his brother, the strong, heavy smell of his mother and her milk, revived in his nostrils.

When he had sucked his fill, his body grew warm and comfortable. A liquid warmth flowed through his veins, his head separated heavily from his mother's breast, his body quivered with pleasure from head to tail, and a deep sleep followed. What pleasure greater than this was possible? To instinctively press his paws against his mother's breast, and with no special effort the milk would come out. The fluffy body of his brother, his mother's voice, all of this was full of pleasure. He remembered his old wooden doghouse, the games he used to play in that green garden with his brother.

He would bite his floppy ears, they would fall on the ground, get up, run; and later he found another playmate, too, his owner's son. He would run after him at the end of the garden, bark, take his clothes in his teeth. In particular, he could never forget the caresses his owner had given him, the lumps of sugar he had eaten from his hand. Still, he liked his owner's son better, because they had been playmates and the boy would never hit him. Later, he suddenly lost his mother and brother. Only his owner and his owner's wife and son and an old servant were left. How well he distinguished their smells and recognized from afar the sound of their footsteps. At lunch and supper he would circle the table and smell the food, and sometimes against her husband's will his owner's wife would kindly give him a titbit. Then the old servant would come, calling, "Pat... Pat..." and would pour his food in a special dish which was beside his doghouse.

Natural needs caused Pat's misfortune, because his owner wouldn't let him out of the house to go after female dogs. As luck would have it, one autumn day his owner and two other people who often came to their house and whom Pat knew got in the car. Pat had travelled with his owner in the car several times, but today he was agitated. After several hours of driving, they got out in Varamin Square. His owner and the two others passed through the alley beside the tower, but suddenly there was the unexpected stench of a bitch, that special smell that Pat was searching for, and all at once he was driven crazy. He sniffed in different places and finally entered a garden through a water channel.

Twice near dusk the sound of his owner's voice calling "Pat! Pat!" reached his ears. Was it really his voice, or was the echo of his voice sounding in Pat's ears?

Although his owner's voice had a strong hold on Pat, because it reminded him of all the obligations and duties that he owed him, still a power superior to that of the outside world compelled him to stay with the bitch. He felt that his ears had grown too heavy and dull to hear sounds outside himself. Strong feelings had awakened in him, and the smell of the bitch was so powerful that he felt giddy.

All his muscles, all his body and his senses, were beyond his control, so that they were no longer obedient to him. But it wasn't long until people came with sticks and shovel handles and shouts and drove him out through the water channel.

Dizzy, giddy and tired, but light and relieved, as soon as Pat came to himself he went to look for his master. In several side alleys a faint odour of him had remained. He looked everywhere, leaving traces of himself at intervals. He went as far as the ruins outside the town. Then Pat returned because he realized that his owner had gone back to the square, but from there his faint scent got lost among others. Had his owner gone and left him behind? He felt agitated and fearful. How could Pat live without his master, his God? For his owner was like a god to him. But at the same time he was certain that his owner would come to look for him. Frightened, he began running up and down the roads; his efforts were wasted.

When night fell he returned to the square, tired and exhausted. There was no trace of his master. He circled the village a few more times, finally going to the water channel that led to the bitch, but the entrance had been blocked with rocks. With peculiar enthusiasm, Pat dug at the ground with his paws in the hope of being able to enter the garden, but it was impossible. Disappointed, he napped there.

In the middle of the night Pat jumped awake at the sound of his own moans. Frightened, he got up. He prowled about in the alleys helpless and perplexed. At length he felt very hungry. When he returned to the square, the odour of different foods reached his nostrils. The smells of leftover meat, fresh bread and yoghurt were all mingled together, but at the same time he felt guilty for trespassing. He must beg from these people who resembled his owner, and if another rival shouldn't turn up to drive him out, little by little he could obtain the right to this territory. Perhaps one of these beings who had food would take care of him.

Trembling with fear, he went cautiously towards the bakery, which had just opened and from which the strong smell of baked bread diffused in the air. Somebody with a loaf of bread under his arm said to him, "Come… Come!" How strange his voice sounded in Pat's ears! The man threw a piece of warm bread in front of him. After hesitating a moment, Pat ate the bread and wagged his tail. The man put the bread down on the shop bench. Fearfully and cautiously, he laid his hand on Pat's head. Then, with both hands, he undid Pat's collar. How comfortable Pat felt: it was as if all the responsibilities, obligations, and duties were lifted from his shoulders. But when he wagged his tail again and went towards the shop owner, he met a heavy kick in the side and retreated, moaning. The owner of the shop went and carefully dipped his hands in the water of the ditch. Pat still recognized his collar hanging in front of the shop.

From that day on, aside from kicks, rocks, and beatings from the club, Pat had earned nothing from these people. It was as if they were his sworn enemies and took pleasure in torturing him.

Pat felt that he had entered a new world which didn't belong to him and in which no one understood his feelings. He passed the first few days with difficulty, but he adjusted by and by. On the right-hand side of the alley, where it turned, he discovered a place where rubbish was thrown. In the refuse many delicious titbits could be found, such as bones, fat, skin, fish heads, and many other things which he couldn't identify. After scavenging he would spend the rest of the day in front of the butcher's shop and the bakery. His eyes were glued to the butcher's hands, but he received more blows than delicious morsels. Eventually he came to terms with his new way of life. Of his past life only a handful of hazy, vague memories and some scents remained, and whenever things were particularly hard for him, he would find a measure of consolation and escape in this lost heaven of his, while involuntarily the memories of that time would take shape before his eyes.

But the thing that tortured Pat more than anything else was his need to be fondled. He was like a child who had always been cursed and made a scapegoat, but whose finer feelings had not yet been extinguished. Especially in this new life full of pain and torment, he needed to be caressed more than before. His eyes begged for this fondling, and he was ready to lay down his life for the person who would be kind to him or stroke him on the head. He needed to display his kindness to someone, to sacrifice himself for someone, to show someone his feelings of worship and loyalty, but it seemed that no one would take his part. In every eye he looked at he saw nothing but hatred and mischief. Whatever movement he made to attract the attention of these people, it seemed to rouse their indignation and wrath still more.

While Pat was napping in the water channel, he moaned and woke up several times, as if he were having nightmares. Presently he felt very hungry. He smelt grilled meat. A treacherous hunger tortured his insides so much that he forgot his helplessness and his other pains. He arose with difficulty and went cautiously towards the square.

* * *

At this time, amid noise and dust, a car entered Varamin Square. A man got out of the car, walked towards Pat and patted his head. This man was not his owner. Pat wasn't fooled, because he knew his owner's scent very well. But why had somebody come to caress him? Pat wagged his tail and looked doubtfully at the man. Hadn't he been tricked? But there was no longer a collar around his neck to pat him for. The man turned and patted him once more. Pat followed him, his surprise increasing, because the man went inside a shop that Pat knew well, from which the smell of food came. The man sat on a bench by the wall. He was served warm bread, yoghurt, eggs and other things. He dipped pieces of bread in the yoghurt and threw them in front of Pat. At first hurriedly, then more slowly, Pat ate the bread, his good-natured hazel eyes full of unhappiness riveted to the man's face in thanks, his tail wagging. Was he awake, or was he dreaming? Pat ate a full meal without being interrupted by blows. Could it be possible that he had found a new owner? In spite of the heat, the man got up. He went down the same alley to the tower, paused there a bit, then passed through winding alleys. Pat followed him, until he went out of the village. The man went to the same ruin, which had several walls, to which his owner had gone. Perhaps these people, too, followed the scent of their females? Pat waited for him in the shade of the wall. Then they returned to the square by a different route.

The man laid his hand on Pat's head again and after a brief walk around the square, he went and got into one of those cars that Pat knew. Pat didn't have the courage to jump up. He sat next to the car and looked at the men.

All at once the car started in a cloud of dust. Without hesitation, Pat ran after the car. No, this time he didn't want to let the man get away from him. He panted and in spite of the pain he felt in his body, he leapt up and ran after the car with all his strength. The car left the village behind and passed through fields. Pat reached the car two or three times but then fell back. He had gathered all his strength, and his despair forced him to run as fast as he could. But the car went faster than he did. He had made a mistake. Not only was he unable to reach the car, but he had become weak and broken and suddenly he felt that his muscles were no longer in his control. He was not able to make the slightest move. All his effort had been in vain. He actually didn't know why he had run or where he was going. He had come to a dead end. He stood and panted, his tongue hanging out. It had grown dark before his eyes. His head hanging, he pulled himself laboriously away from the road and went into a ditch beside the field. He lay on the hot moist sand, and with his instinct, which was never deceptive, he felt that he could not move any more from this spot. His head was dizzy. His thoughts and feelings had become vague and dark. He felt a severe pain in his stomach, and his eyes looked glazed over with sickness. In the midst of writhing and spasms, he lost control of his legs little by little. A cold sweat covered his body. It was a mild, intoxicating coolness…

* * *

Near dusk three hungry crows flew over Pat's head. They had smelled him from afar. One of them cautiously landed near him and looked carefully. When it was certain that Pat was not yet completely dead, it flew up again. The three crows had come to tear out his hazel eyes.

The Broken Mirror

(from *Three Drops of Blood*)

ODETTE WAS AS FRESH as the flowers that blossom at the beginning of spring, with a pair of alluring eyes the colour of the sky and blonde hair which always hung in wisps by her cheeks. With a pale, delicate profile she would sit for hours in front of her window. She would cross her legs, read a novel, mend her stockings or do embroidery. But it was when she played the Garizari Waltz on her violin that she pulled at my heartstrings.

The window of my room was opposite the window of Odette's room. How many minutes, hours, and maybe even whole Sundays I would watch her from my window: especially at night when she took off her stockings and got into bed.

In this way a mysterious relationship had developed between us. If I didn't see her for one day, it was as if I had lost something. Some days I would look at her so long that she would get up and close her window. We had been watching each other for two weeks, but Odette's glance was cold and indifferent. She did not smile or make any move to reveal her feelings towards me. Basically her expression was serious and self-contained.

The first time that I came face to face with her was one morning when I had gone to the café at the end of our alley to have breakfast. When I came out, I saw Odette. Her violin case was in her hand and she was going towards the metro. I said hello and she smiled. Then I asked if I could carry her violin case. She nodded her head in answer and said "Thanks". Our acquaintance started with this one word.

From that day on, when we opened our windows, we talked to each other from afar with hand motions and gestures. But it always resulted in our going down to the Luxembourg Gardens and meeting each other. Afterwards we would go to a film or to the theatre, or spend several hours together in some other way. Odette was alone at home. Her stepfather and her mother had gone on a trip, and she remained in Paris because of her job.

She spoke very little. But she had the temperament of a child: she was wilful and stubborn, and sometimes she infuriated me. We had been friends for two months. One day we decided to go that evening to the Friday market at Neuilly. That night Odette wore her new blue dress and seemed happier than usual. When we came out of the restaurant, she spoke of her life all the way on the metro, until we came out opposite Luna Park.

A large crowd was coming and going. All kinds of amusements were spread along the street. Entertainers were performing. There were shooting games, lottery games, sweet-sellers, a circus, small electric cars that went around a track, balloons which revolved around themselves, rides, and various exhibits. The sounds of girls' screams, conversation, laughter, murmuring, and the noise of motors and different sorts of music were mingled together.

We decided to go on a car ride. It was a train of cars which went around in a circle and when it was moving, a cloth would cover it, making it look like a green worm. When we wanted to get on, Odette gave her gloves and purse to me so they wouldn't fall during the ride. We sat close beside each other. The ride started and the green cover slowly rose and hid us from the eyes of the onlookers for five minutes.

When the cover fell back, our lips were still pressed together. I was kissing Odette and she was not holding back. Then we got out, and while walking, she told me that this was only the third time she had come to the Friday market, because her mother had forbidden her. We went to look at several other places. It was midnight when, tired and worn out, we finally started to return. But Odette didn't want to leave. She stopped at each show, and I was obliged to wait. Two or three times I dragged her by the arm, and she was forced to come with me, until she stopped in front of the stand of somebody who was selling Gillette razor blades. He was delivering a speech and demonstrating how good they were and inviting people to buy. This time I became really infuriated. I pulled her arm hard and said, "This has nothing to do with women." But she pulled her arm away and said, "I know. I still want to watch."

I went towards the metro without answering her. When I got home, the alley was deserted and Odette's window was dark. I went into my room and turned on the light. I opened the window, and since I wasn't sleepy, I read for a while. It was one in the morning. I went to close the window and go to sleep. I saw that Odette had come and was standing in the alley by the street light beneath her window. I was surprised by her behaviour. I slammed the window shut. As I started to undress, I realized that Odette's beaded purse and her gloves were in my pocket and I knew that her money and door key were in the purse. I tied them together and dropped them out the window.

Three weeks passed and during all that time I paid no attention to her. When her window opened, I closed mine. In the meantime it happened that I had to make a trip to London. The day before I left for England, I ran into Odette at the end of the alley, going towards the metro with her violin case in her hand. After saying hello and exchanging a few pleasantries, I told her about my trip and apologized for my behaviour that night. Odette coldly opened her beaded purse and handed me a small mirror which was broken in the middle. She said, "This happened that night you threw my purse out of the window. You know this will bring bad luck."

I laughed in answer and called her superstitious, and promised her that I would see her again before I left, but unfortunately I couldn't make it.

After I had been in London about a month I received this letter from Odette:

Paris, 21st September 1930

Dearest Jamshid,
You don't know how lonely I am. This loneliness hurts me. I want to say a few words to you tonight, because when I write to you it's as if I am speaking with you. If I address you familiarly please excuse me. If you only knew how much I am suffering!

How long the days are – the hands of the clock move so slowly that I don't know what to do. Does time seem so slow to you too? Perhaps you've met a girl there, although I'm sure that your head is always in a book, just the way you were in Paris, in that tiny room that is always before my eyes. Now a Chinese student has moved in, but I've hung a heavy curtain across my window so that I won't be able to see out, because the person that I loved isn't there. It's just like the refrain in the ballad says: "A bird that's gone to another land won't come back."

Yesterday Helen and I went walking in the Luxembourg Gardens. When we got to that stone bench, I remembered the day we sat on the same bench and you spoke of your country, and how you made me all those promises and I believed them. And now I've become an object of ridicule to my friends, and people talk about me. I always play the Garizari Waltz to remember you. The picture we took in the Bois de Vincennes is on my table. When I look at your picture it reassures me. I say to myself, "No, this picture doesn't fool me!" But alas, I don't know if you share my feelings or not. But ever since that night my mirror broke, the very mirror that you gave me yourself, my heart has been warning me of some unfortunate event. The last day that we saw each other, when you said that you were going to England, my heart told me that you were going very far and we would never see each other again. And the thing that I worried about has happened. Madame Burle asked, "Why are you so sad?" and she wanted to take me to Brittany, but I didn't go with her, because I knew that I would get worse.

Never mind – what's over is over. If I'm sounding cross, it's because I'm feeling depressed. Please forgive me, and if I've harassed you I hope you will forget me. You'll tear up my letters, won't you, Jimmy?

If you knew how much pain and sorrow I'm in at this moment. I'm tired of everything. I'm disillusioned with my daily work, although it wasn't like this before. You know, I can't bear to be left hanging any longer, even if it becomes a cause of grief to others. All of their sorrow can't equal mine. I have decided to leave Paris on Sunday. I'll take the six-thirty train and go to Calais, the last city that you passed through. Then I'll see the blue water of the ocean. That water washes all misfortunes away. Every moment its colour changes, and it laps the sandy shore with its sad, enchanting murmur. It foams. The sand nibbles the foam and swallows it and then those very same waves will take my last thoughts with them, because when death smiles at someone, it draws him to it with this smile. Perhaps you will say that she couldn't do such a thing, but you will see that I don't tell lies.

Accept my distant kisses,

Odette Lasour

I sent two letters in answer to Odette, but one of them remained unanswered and the second was stamped "Return to Sender" and came back to me.

The next year, when I returned to Paris, I went as quickly as possible to Rue Saint Jacques, where my old house was. From my room a Chinese student was whistling the Garizari Waltz. But the window of Odette's room was shut, and a paper had been stuck on the front door which said "To Let".

Davoud the Hunchback

(from *Buried Alive*)

"NO, NO. I will never follow this path. I must completely close my eyes to it. It brings happiness to others, while for me it's full of pain and torture. Never, never…" Davoud was talking to himself, striking the ground with the short yellow-coloured stick which he had in his hand, and with which he struggled along, as if he kept his balance with difficulty. His big head was sunken between his thin shoulders onto his protruding chest. From the front he appeared hollow, terrible, and repulsive: thin withered lips, thin curved eyebrows, drooping eyelashes, sallow colour, prominent bony cheeks. But when someone looked at him from a distance with his coat covering his hump-back, his long disproportionate hands, his big hat pulled down on his head, and especially the serious attitude he assumed, hitting his stick with force on the ground, he seemed rather more laughable.

From the intersection of Pahlavi Avenue he had turned into a street out of the city and was going towards the Government Gate. It was near dusk and the weather was slightly warm. On the left, in the vague light of the sunset, the mud-covered walls and brick columns thrust their heads towards the sky in silence. On the right was a gully that had just been filled and next to that at intervals, half built brick houses were visible. Here it was fairly empty, and sometimes a car or a droshky would pass which raised a little dust into the air even though water had been sprinkled on the road. Saplings had been planted on both sides of the street, by the gutter.

He was thinking that from the beginning of his childhood up to the present he had always been the object of other people's ridicule or pity. He remembered that the first time the teacher in the history class said the inhabitants of Sparta used to kill deformed children all the students turned around and looked at him, and it had made him feel strange. But now he wished that this law had been enforced everywhere in the world, or at least that, as in most places, they would have banned syphilitic people from marrying, since he knew that all this was his father's fault. The scene of his father's death, the pale face, bony cheeks, sunken blue eyes, half-open mouth, passed before his eyes just as he had seen it: his old syphilitic father, who had taken a young wife and all of whose children had been born blind or lame. One of his brothers who had survived was dumb and an idiot and had died two years ago. He would say to himself, "Maybe they were the lucky ones!"

But he remained alive, weary of himself and others, and everyone avoided him. He had grown somewhat accustomed to living for ever a life apart. From childhood in school he was left out of sports, jokes, races, ball games, leapfrog, tag and all the things which brought about the happiness of his classmates. During playtime he would crouch in the corner of the school playground holding a book in front of his face and watching the children stealthily from behind it. But there was a time when he truly worked, and he wanted to find superiority over the others at least through study. Day and night he worked, and because of this one or two of the lazy students became friendly with him, because they wanted to copy his exercises and his solutions to maths problems. But he knew that their friendship was insincere and was to their advantage, since he saw that the students tried hard to be friends with Hasan Khan, who was handsome, well-built, and wore nice clothes. Only one or two people among the teachers showed Davoud any consideration and attention, and this wasn't for his work but because they pitied him, since even with all his labour and hardship he couldn't complete his work.

Now he remained empty handed. Everyone avoided him. His acquaintances would be embarrassed to walk with him, women would say "See the hunchback!" This made him more angry than anything else.

Twice, several years before, he had asked for a girl's hand. Both times the women had ridiculed him. By coincidence one of them, Zibandeh, lived near here in Fisherabad. They had seen each other several times, and they had even talked to each other. In the afternoons when he came home from school he used to come here to see her. The only thing he could remember was that she had a mole by her lip. Later when he sent his aunt to ask for her hand that same girl had ridiculed him and said, "But is there a dearth of men, that I should become the wife of a hunchback?" No matter how much her father and mother had beaten her, she hadn't accepted. She kept saying, "But is there a dearth of men?" But Davoud still loved her, and this counted as the best memory of his youth. Even now, wittingly or unwittingly, he mostly wandered here, and the past memories would become fresh again before his eyes. He was disappointed in everything. Mostly he went for walks alone and kept aloof from crowds because he suspected that everyone who laughed or talked quietly to his friend was talking about him, was making fun of him. With his brown staring eyes and fierce attitude he would laboriously move his neck and the upper half of his body and would pass on looking down contemptuously. When he went out all his senses were attuned to others, all the muscles of his face were tense. He wanted to know other people's opinion about him.

He was passing slowly by the side of a gutter and sometimes he stirred the water with the end of his stick. His thoughts were frenzied and distressed. He saw a white dog with long hair who lifted its head because of the sound of his stick hitting against a rock, and it looked at him as if it was sick or on the verge of death. It couldn't move from its place and once again its head dropped to the ground. He stooped down with difficulty. In the light of the moon their eyes met. A strange thought occurred to him: he felt that this was the first time that he had seen a simple and sincere look and that both of them were unfortunate and unwanted, rejected and useless, driven out from human society. He wanted to sit by this dog, who had dragged its misery out of the city and had hidden it from men's eyes, and take it in his embrace, press its head to his protruding chest. But he thought that if someone passed by here and saw, he would make fun of him even more. It was dusk. He passed by the Yusef Abad Gate. He looked at the circle of the incandescent moon, which in the calm of this sorrowful and tender evening had come up from the shore of the sky. He looked at the half-built houses, the piles of bricks which they had heaped on each other, the sleepy background of the city, the tin roofs of the houses, the blue-coloured mountain. Grey blurred curtains were passing before his eyes. No one could be seen, near or far. The distant muffled sound of singing was coming from the other side of the gully. He lifted his head with difficulty. He was tired, extremely sad and unhappy, and his eyes burned. It was as if his head was too heavy for his body. Davoud left his walking stick by the side of the ditch and went over to the other side.

Without intending to, he walked towards the rocks and sat down beside the road. Suddenly he became aware of a woman in a *chador* who was sitting near him beside the ditch. His heartbeat speeded up. Suddenly the woman turned her head and said with a smile, "Hushang! Where were you until now?" Davoud was surprised by the women's easy tone, surprised that she had seen him and hadn't been startled. It was as if he had been given the world. From her question it was evident that she wanted to talk with him, but what was she doing here at this time of night? Was she decent? Maybe she was in love. He took a chance, saying to himself, come what may, at least I've found someone to talk to, maybe she'll give me comfort. As if he had no control over his own tongue he said, "Miss, are you alone? I'm alone too. I'm always alone. I've been alone all my life."

His words weren't yet finished when the woman, wearing sunglasses, turned her head again and said, "Then who are you? I thought it was Hushang. Whenever he meets me, he tries to be funny."

Davoud didn't follow much of this last sentence, and he didn't understand what the women meant. But he didn't expect to, either. It had been a long time since any woman had talked to him. He saw this woman was pretty. Cold sweat streamed down his body. With difficulty he said, "No, miss, I'm not Hushang. My name is Davoud."

The woman answered with a smile, "I can't see you – my eyes hurt. Aha, Davoud!... Davoud the Hunch..." she bit her lip. "I'm Zibandeh. Don't you know me?" The curled hair which had covered her cheek moved, and Davoud saw the black mole at the corner of her lip. He throbbed from chest to throat. Drops of sweat rolled down his forehead. He looked around. No one was there. The sound of the singing had come near. His heart beat. It beat so fast that he couldn't breathe. Without saying anything, trembling from head to foot, he got up. Sobs choked his throat. He picked up his cane. With heavy steps rising and falling he went back the same way he had come and with a scratchy voice he whispered to himself, "That was Zibandeh! She didn't see me... Maybe Hushang was her fiancé or husband... Who knows? No... Never... I must close my eyes completely!... No, no I can't any more..."

He pulled himself along to the side of the same dog that he had seen, sat and pressed its head to his protruding chest. But the dog was dead.

Madeline

(from *Buried Alive*)

T HE NIGHT BEFORE LAST I was there, in that small living room. Her mother and her sister were there too. The mother wore a grey dress and the daughters wore red dresses. The furniture, too, was of red velvet. I was resting my elbow on the piano and looking at them. There was silence except for the record player, from which was coming the stirring, sorrowful song of 'The Volga Boatman'. The wind roared; drops of rain beat against the window. The rain trickled, and with a constant sound blended with the melody of the record. Madeleine sat in front of me, thoughtful and gloomy, with her head leaning on her hand, listening. I looked stealthily at her brown, curly hair, bare arms, lively, childish neck and profile. This mood she was in struck me as being artificial. I thought she should always run, play and joke. I couldn't imagine that thoughts came to her or that it was possible for her also to be sad. I liked her childish and unrestrained attitude.

This was the third time that I had met her. I was introduced to her first at the seaside, but she had changed a lot since then. She and her sister had been wearing bathing suits. They had been carefree, with cheerful faces. She was childlike, mischievous, with shining eyes. It was near dusk. The waves of the sea, the music from the casino – I remembered everything. Now they wore the reddish purple dresses that were stylish this year, whose long skirts covered them to the ankles. They looked aged, apprehensive and seemed preoccupied with life's problems.

The record stopped, cutting off the distant, choked tune which was not unlike the waves of the sea. To liven things up, their mother spoke of school and the activities of her daughters. She said that Madeleine was a top student in art. Her sister winked at me. I smiled outwardly and gave short, perfunctory answers to their questions. But my thoughts were elsewhere. I was reviewing from the beginning my acquaintance with them. About two months ago, during the summer vacation just gone by, I had gone to the seaside with one of my friends. It was warm and crowded. We went to Trouville. In front of the railway station we took a bus. Through the forest beside the sea, our bus slipped among hundreds of cars, amid the sound of horns and the smell of oil and gasoline diffused in the air. The bus shook. Sometimes a view of sea appeared beyond the trees.

Finally we got off at one of the stations, Ville Royale. We passed through several alleys lined on each side with walls of stone and mud. We arrived at a small bun-shaped beach which had been built up on a rise by the sea. In the small square opposite the sea, a small casino could be seen. Around it, on the hills, houses and small villas had been built. Lower down, near the water, there was sand, and beyond that there were the waves. There, small children, alone or with their mothers, were busy playing ball or digging in the sand. A handful of men and women in bathing suits were swimming or were running into the water a little way and coming back. Others, on the sand, were sitting or lying in the sun. Old men lounged under striped umbrellas, reading newspapers and furtively watching the women. We, too, went in front of the casino, with our backs to the water, and sat on the long, wide edge of the sea wall. The sun was about to set. The tide was coming in, and the waves pounded on the shore. The sun sparkled on the waves in triangles of light. A big black ship could be seen going through the mist to the port of Le Havre. The air became slightly cool. The people near the water were coming up by and by. At this point my friend got up and shook hands with two girls who had come near us. He introduced me. They came and sat beside us on the high edge of the sea wall. Madeleine, with a large ball in her hand, sat beside me and started to talk as if she had known me for years. Sometimes she would get up and play with the ball in her hands and then she would come and sit beside me again. I'd tease her, grab the ball from her and then give it back to her and our hands would touch. Slowly we pressed each other's hands. Her hand had a delicate warmth. I glanced furtively at her breasts, her bare legs, her head and neck. I thought to myself how nice it would be to lay my head on her breast and sleep right there by the sea. The sun set and a pale moonlight gave this small, remote beach an intimate, family atmosphere. Suddenly a dance tune sounded from the casino. Madeleine, her hand in mine, started to sing an American dance tune, 'Mississippi'. I pressed her hand. From a distance the brightness of the lighthouse cast a half circle of light on the water. The roar of the water hitting the shore could be heard. People's shadows were passing in front of us.

At this point, while these images were passing before my eyes, her mother came and sat at the piano. I moved aside. All at once I saw Madeleine get up like a sleepwalker. She went and searched through the sheet music scattered on the table, separated one piece, took it and put it in front of her mother, and came with a smile to stand near me. Her mother started to play the piano. Madeleine sang softly. It was the same dance tune that I had heard in the Ville Royale – the same 'Mississippi'.

Dash Akol

(from *Three Drops of Blood*)

E VERYONE IN SHIRAZ KNEW that Dash Akol and Kaka Rostam hated each other. One day Dash Akol was squatting on a bench at the Domil Teahouse, his old hangout. Beside him was a quail cage with a red cover over it. With his fingertip he twirled a piece of ice around in a bowl of water. Suddenly Kaka Rostam came in. He threw Dash Akol a contemptuous look and with his hand in his sash went and sat on the opposite bench. Then he turned to the teahouse boy and said "S-s-son, bri-bring some tea."

Dash threw a look full of meaning at the boy, so that he became apprehensive and ignored Kaka's order. The boy took the dirty teacups out of a bronze bowl and dipped them into a bucket of water. Then one by one he dried them very slowly. A scratchy sound arose from the rubbing of the towel against the cups.

This snub made Kaka Rostam furious. Once again he yelled, "A-a-are you deaf? I-I-I'm talking to you!"

The boy looked at Dash Akol with an uncertain smile, and Kaka Rostam snarled, "D-d-devil take them. P-p-people who th-th-think they're so great will c-c-come tonight and p-prove it, if they're any g-g-good."

Dash Akol was whirling the ice around in the bowl, noticing the situation slyly. He laughed impudently, showing a row of strong white teeth shining beneath his henna-dyed moustache, and said, "Cowards brag, but pretty soon it will be evident who's the better man."

Everyone laughed. They didn't laugh at Kaka Rostam's stuttering, because they knew he stuttered, but because Dash Akol was very well known in the town. No "tough guys" could be found who hadn't tasted his blows. Whenever he would drink a bottle of double distilled vodka in Nolla Ashaq's house and then take on all comers at the corner of Sare Dozak, he would be more than a match for Kaka Rostam. Even fellows much stronger than Kaka Rostam wouldn't dare

75

to fight him. Kaka himself knew that he was not a match for Dash Akol, because he had been wounded twice at his hands, and three or four times Dash Akol had overpowered him and sat on his chest. Unluckily, several nights before, Kaka Rostam had seen the corner empty and had started boasting. Dash Akol arrived unexpectedly, like an avenging angel, and heaped insults on his head. Dash had said to him, "Kaka, you sissy, it seems you've been smoking too much opium… It's made you pretty high. You know what, you'd better stop this vile, dastardly behaviour. You're acting like a hoodlum, and you aren't a bit ashamed. This certainly is some kind of beggary that you've picked up as a business, I swear if you get really drunk like this again I'll smoke your moustache off. I'll split you in half."

Then Kaka Rostam had set off with his tail between his legs. But he developed a grudge against Dash Akol, and he was always looking for an excuse to take revenge.

Everybody in Shiraz liked Dash Akol, because, although he challenged any man at the corner of Sare Dozak, he didn't bother women and children. On the contrary, he was kind to people, and if some miserable fellow bothered a woman or threatened someone, he wouldn't be able to get away from Dash Akol in one piece. Dash Akol was usually seen to help people. He was benevolent, and if he was in the mood he would even carry people's loads home for them. But he couldn't stand to be second to anyone, especially not to Kaka Rostam, that opium-smoking, phoney busybody.

Kaka Rostam sat infuriated by this contempt which had been shown him. He chewed his moustache, and he was so angry that if someone had stabbed him, he wouldn't have bled. After a few minutes, when the volley of laughter died down, everyone was still except the teahouse boy. Wearing a collarless shirt, nightcap, and black twill trousers, the boy held his hand over his stomach, and writhed with laughter, nearly worn out. Most of the others were laughing at his laughter. Kaka Rostam lost his temper. He reached out and picked up the crystal sugar bowl and threw it at the boy. But the sugar bowl hit the samovar, which rolled off the bench to the floor together with the teapot and broke several cups. Then Kaka Rostam got up, his face flushed with anger, and went out of the teahouse.

The teahouse keeper examined the samovar with a distressed air and said, "Rostam, the legendary hero, had only one suit of armour.

All I had was this dilapidated samovar." He uttered this in a sad tone, but because of the allusion to Rostam, people laughed even harder. The teahouse keeper attacked the boy in frustration, but Dash Akol with a smile reached into his pocket, pulled out a bag of money, and threw it to him.

The teahouse keeper picked up the bag, hefted it, and smiled.

At this point a man with a velvet vest, loose trousers, and a felt hat rushed headlong into the teahouse. He glanced around, went up to Dash Akol, greeted him, and said, "Hajji Samad is dead."

Dash Akol raised his head and said, "God bless him!"

"But don't you know he's left a will?"

"I don't live off the dead. Go and tell somebody who does."

"But he's made you the executor of his will."

As if these words awakened Dash Akol from his indifference, once again he looked the man up and down, rubbing his hand on his forehead. His egg-shaped hat was pushed back, showing his two-toned forehead, half of which was burnt brown by the sun and half of which had remained white from being under the hat. Then he shook his head, took out his inlaid pipe, slowly filled it with tobacco, tapped it with his thumb, lit it, and said, "God bless Hajji now that it's over, but that wasn't a good thing he did. He's thrown me into a sea of trouble. Well, you go, I'll come after."

The person who had entered was Hajji Samad's foreman. Taking long steps, he went out of the door. Dash Akol frowned in thought. He puffed on his pipe reflectively. Somehow it was as if dark clouds had suddenly stifled the cheerful, happy atmosphere of the teahouse. After Dash Akol emptied the ashes from his pipe he got up, gave the quail cage to the boy, and went out of the teahouse.

When Dash Akol entered Hajji Samad's courtyard, the reading of the Koran was over. There were only a few readers left and some men to carry the Koran who were grumbling over their fee. After waiting a few minutes by the fountain, he was taken into a big room whose sash windows opened onto the courtyard. Hajji's wife came and stood behind a curtain, and after the usual greetings and pleasantries Dash Akol sat on a mattress and said, "Ma'am, may God keep you in good health. May God bless your children." The woman said in a choked voice, "On the night that Hajji fell ill, they brought His Eminence the Imam* Jomeh to pray at his bedside, and in the presence of all Hajji announced you as the executor of his will. Probably you knew Hajji from before?"

"We met five years ago on a trip to Kazeroon."

"Hajji, God bless him, always said that if there was only one real man, it was Dash Akol."

"Ma'am, I like my freedom more than anything else, but now that I've been obliged by the dead, I swear by this ray of light that if I don't die first, I'll show those cabbage heads."

Then as he lifted his head, he saw from between two curtains a girl with a glowing face and alluring black eyes. They had looked at each other for not even a moment when the girl, as if she felt embarrassed, dropped the curtain and stepped back. Was she pretty? Perhaps. In any case her alluring eyes did their work and Dash Akol was ravished. He blushed and dropped his head.

It was Marjan, the daughter of Hajji Samad. She had come out of curiosity to see the famous Dash Akol, who was now her guardian.

The next day Dash Akol began to work on Hajji's affairs. With an expert in second-hand goods, two men from the neighbourhood, and a secretary, he carefully registered and inventoried everything. Whatever was extra he put in the storeroom, locking and sealing the door. Whatever would bring anything he sold. He had the deeds of Hajji's lands read to him. He collected what was owing to Hajji and paid his debts. All of these things were accomplished in two days and two nights. On the third night, tired and worn out, Dash Akol was passing near Sayyed Haj Qarib Square on his way home. On the way he ran into Imam Qoli Chalengar, who said, "Now it's been two nights that Kaka Rostam has been expecting you. Last night he was saying that you left him up in the air. He says that you've got a taste of high life and you've forgotten your promise."

Dash Akol remembered well that three days before in the Domile Teahouse Kaka Rostam had challenged him, but since he knew what kind of man Kaka was and knew that Kaka had plotted with Imam Qoli to shame him, he didn't pay any attention and continued on his way. On the way all his senses were concentrated on Marjan. No matter how much he wanted to drive her face away from before his eyes, it would take shape more firmly in his imagination.

Dash Akol was a big man of thirty-five, but he wasn't good looking. Seeing him for the first time would dampen anyone's spirits, but if someone sat and talked to him or heard the stories about his life which people were always telling, he would become fascinated. When one didn't consider the sword scars going from left to right, Dash Akol had a noble and arresting face: hazel eyes, thick black eyebrows, broad cheeks, narrow nose, black beard and moustache. But his scars spoilt everything. On his cheeks and forehead were the marks of sword wounds which had healed badly, leaving raw-looking furrows on his face. Worst of all, one of them had drawn down the corner of his left eye.

His father was one of the great landowners of Fars Province. When he died all his property went to his only son. But Dash Akol took life easy and spent money recklessly. He didn't consider wealth and property important. He passed his life freely and generously. He had no ties in life, and he generously gave all his possessions to the poor and empty-handed. Either he would drink vodka and raise hell in the streets or he would spend his time getting together with a handful of friends who had become his parasites. All his faults and virtues were confined to these activities, but the thing which seemed surprising was that the subject of love had never come up for him. Although several times his friends had talked him into coming to bull sessions, he never took part in the conversation. But from the day he became Hajji Samdad's executor and saw Marjan, his life changed completely. On the one hand he considered himself obliged to the dead and under a burden of responsibility; on the other hand, he had lost his heart to Marjan. But the responsibility weighed on him more than anything. He had wasted his own wealth and had also squandered part of his own inheritance through carelessness. Now every day from early morning when he awoke he thought only of how to increase the income of Hajji's estate. He moved Hajji's wife and children into a smaller house. He rented out their private house. He brought a tutor for the children. He invested their money, and from morning until night he was busy chasing after Hajji's affairs.

From this time on Dash Akol completely gave up prowling around at night and daring others to fight. He lost interest in his friends, and he lost his old enthusiasm. But all the men who had been his rivals, incited by the mullahs who felt themselves cheated of Hajji's wealth, found a little legroom for themselves, and they made sarcastic remarks about Dash Akol. Talk of him filled the teahouses and other gathering places. At the Pachenar Teahouse people often discussed Dash Akol, saying things like, "Talking about Dash Akol – he doesn't dare any more, his tongue's frozen. That dirty dog. They really got rid of him. Now he sniffs around Hajji's door. Seems like he is scrounging something. Now when he comes around Sare Dozak he drops his tail between his legs and slinks by."

Kaka Rostam, carrying a grudge in his heart, stuttered, "Th-th-there's no f-f-f-fool like an old fool. The guy has f-f-fallen in love with Ha-Ha-Hajji Samad's daughter! He's sh-sh-sh-sheathed his butter knife! He's thrown d-d-dirt in people's eyes. He m-m-made a false r-r-r-reputation for himself and got to be Hajji's e-e-e-executor. He'll steal them all b-b-b-blind. Lucky d-d-dog."

People no longer put stock in Dash Akol and no longer held him in awe. In every place he entered, people were whispering in each other's ears and making fun of him. Dash Akol heard this talk here and there, but he didn't show it and didn't pay any attention, because his love of Marjan had grown so strong within him and had so upset him that he had no thought except for her.

At night he would drink alcohol in his distress, and he had a parrot to amuse himself with. He sat in front of the cage and told his grievances to the parrot. If Dash Akol asked for Marjan's hand, her mother would gladly give Marjan to him. But on the other hand, he didn't want to become tied to a wife and child, he wanted to be free, just as he had been raised. Besides, he suspected that if he married the girl who had been put into his keeping, he would be doing something wrong. What was worse than everything else was that every night he would look at his drooping eye, and in a rough tone he would say aloud, "Maybe she doesn't like me; maybe she'll find a handsome young husband. No, it's not a manly thing to do... She's fourteen years old and I'm forty... But what shall I do? This love is killing me. Marjan... You've killed me... Who shall I tell... Marjan... Leaving you has destroyed me!"

Tears welled up in his eyes and he drank glass after glass of vodka. Then, with a headache, he fell asleep in his chair.

But at midnight, when the city of Shiraz, with its twisting alleys, exhilarating gardens, and purple wines, went to sleep; when the quiet, mysterious stars were winking at each other in the pitch black sky; when Marjan with her rosy cheeks was breathing softly in her bed and the day's events were passing before her eyes, it was at that time that the real Dash Akol, the natural Dash Akol, with all his feelings, fancies, and desires, with no embarrassment, would come out of the shell which the etiquette and customs of society had built around him. It was then that he would come out of the thoughts which had been inculcated in him since childhood; and freely he hugged Marjan tight and felt her slow heartbeat, her fiery lips and her soft body, and he covered her cheeks with kisses. But when he leapt awake he would curse himself, and curse life, and like a madman he paced up and down his room. He muttered to himself, and in order to kill the thought of love in him, he would busy himself for the rest of the day with running after and taking care of Hajji's affairs.

But an important event, one which should not have happened, took place: a husband appeared for Marjan, and what a husband, who was both older and less attractive than Dash Akol. At this event Dash Akol didn't turn a hair. On the contrary, with extreme contentment he busied himself preparing the trousseau, and he organized a fitting celebration for the wedding night. He took Hajji's wife and children to their own home again and designated the large room with sash windows for entertaining the male guests. All the important people, the merchants and dignitaries of Shiraz, were invited to the festivities.

That day at five in the afternoon, when the guests were sitting around the room cheek by jowl on the priceless carpets and rugs and the big wooden trays of sweets and fruit had been placed in front of them, Dash Akol entered, with his old rough appearance and manner, but with his unruly hair combed and wearing new clothes, a striped robe, a sword belt, a sash, black trousers, cloth shoes, and a hat. Three other people entered behind him with notebooks and pads. All the guests looked him up and down. With long steps Dash Akol went up to His Eminence the Imam Jomeh, and said, "Sir, Hajji, God bless him, made his will and threw me into a sea of trouble for seven years. His youngest son, who was five years old, is now twelve. These are the accounts of Hajji's property." He pointed to the three people standing beside him. "Until today, whatever has been spent, including the expenses of this evening, I have paid from my own pocket. From now on I will go my way, and they will go theirs!"

When he reached this point he stifled a sob. Then without adding anything or waiting for an answer, he dropped his head and with his eyes full of tears went out of the door. In the alley he breathed a sigh of relief. He felt that he had become free and that the burden of responsibility had been lifted from his shoulders, but his heart was broken. He took long, careless steps. As he walked, he recognized the house of the Jewish vodka maker, Mullah Ashaq. Without hesitation he went down the damp steps and entered an old, sooty courtyard which was surrounded by small dirty rooms with windows full of holes like beehives and whose fountain was covered with moss. The smells of fermentation, of feathers, and of old cellars diffused in the air. Mullah Ashaq, skinny, with a dirty nightcap, a goatee beard and covetous eyes, came forwards, laughing artificially.

Dash Akol said gloomily, "By your moustache, give me a bottle of the best to refresh my throat." Mullah Ashaq nodded his head, went down the cellar steps, and after a few minutes came up with a bottle. Dash Akol took the bottle from his hand. He hit the neck against a pillar. The top broke off, and he drained half the bottle. Tears gathered in his eyes, he stifled a cough, and wiped his mouth on the back of his hand. Mullah Ashaq's son, who was a sallow, scrawny, dirty child, with a swollen stomach, an open mouth, and snot hanging on his upper lip, was looking at Dash Akol. Dash Akol put his finger under the lid of a salt cellar which was on a shelf in the courtyard and laid salt on his tongue.

Mullah Ashaq came forwards, clapped Dash Akol on the shoulder and said, "That's the way, fellow." Then he fingered the material of Dash Akol's clothes and said, "What's this you're wearing? This robe is out of style. Whenever you don't want it, I'll pay a good price."

Dash Akol laughed dejectedly. He took some money from his pocket, put it in the palm of Mullah Ashaq's hand, and left the house. It was near dusk. His body was warm, his thoughts were distressed, and his head ached. The alleys were still damp from the afternoon rain and the smell of mud walls and orange blossoms mingled in the air. Marjan's face, her rosy cheeks, black eyes and long lashes, the curly hair on her forehead appeared vaguely and mysteriously before Dash Akol's eyes. He remembered his past life; memories passed before him one by one. He remembered the outing he had made with his friends to the tombs of Saadi and Baba Kouhi. Sometimes he smiled, sometimes he frowned. The one thing he was certain of was that he was afraid of his house – that the state of affairs had become intolerable for him. It was as if his heart had been torn out. He wanted to go far away. He thought that again tonight he would drink and tell his troubles to the parrot! All of life for him had become small, futile, and meaningless. Meanwhile he remembered a poem. Out of boredom he murmured it: "I envy the parties of prisoners / Whose refreshments are chain links." He remembered another poem and recited it a little louder.

> My heart has gone crazy, oh wise ones.
> The crazed man is bound with a chain.
> Bind my heart with a chain of prudence,
> Or its madness will break out again.

He recited this poem in a sad hopeless tone, but as if he had lost interest, or was thinking of something else, he fell silent.

It had grown dark when Dash Akol reached Sare Dozak. This was the same square where in the old days Dash Akol would take on all comers, and no one had dared tangle with him. Without intending it, he went and sat on a stone bench in front of a house. He took out his pipe, filled it, and drew on it slowly. It occurred to him that this place was more run down than it had been; the people looked different to him, just as he himself had changed and broken down. He saw things hazily. His head ached. Suddenly a dark shadow appeared coming towards him, saying, as it approached, "Even the d-d-dark night knows who's the b-b-better man."

Dash Akol recognized Kaka Rostam. He stood up, put his hands on his hips, spat on the ground, and said sarcastically, "God damn your coward father. You think you're the better man? You haven't even learnt where to pee."

Kaka Rostam laughed mockingly, came close, and said, "I-i-i-it's a long t-t-time we haven't seen you around here. Tonight there's a w-w-w-wedding at Hajji's house. Didn't they let y-y-you?…"

Dash Akol interrupted, "God knew what he was doing when he gave you only half a tongue. I'm going to take the other half tonight." He pulled out his sword. Kaka Rostam reached for his sword also. Dash Akol drove his sword into the ground, folded his arms across his chest and said, "Now I dare you to pull that sword out of the ground."

Kaka Rostam suddenly attacked him, but Dash Akol hit the back of his hand so hard that the sword flew out of his grasp. At the sound, a handful of passers-by stopped to watch, but no one dared to come forwards or try to separate them.

Dash Akol said with a smile, "Go on, pick it up, but hold it tighter this time, because tonight I want to settle our accounts!"

Kaka Rostam came forwards with clenched fists and they grappled with each other. They rolled on the ground for half an hour, sweat dripping from their faces, but neither one gained the upper hand. In the middle of the struggle Dash Akol's head hit hard against the cobblestones. He nearly lost consciousness. Kaka Rostam, too, despite the murder in his heart, felt that his power of resistance was exhausted, but suddenly his glance fell on Dash Akol's sword, which was within his reach. With all his strength he pulled it out of the ground and drove it into Dash Akol's side. He pushed it so hard that neither could move any more.

The onlookers ran forwards and lifted up Dash Akol with difficulty. Drops of blood splattered on the ground. He clutched his wound, dragged himself next to the wall a few steps, and fell to the ground again. Then they raised him and carried him to his house.

The next morning, as soon as the news of Dash Akol's wounding reached Hajji Samad's house, Vali Khan, Hajji's oldest son, went to see how he was. When he reached Dash Akol's bedside, he saw him stretched out deathly pale in bed. Bloody froth had bubbled from his lips, and his eyes had darkened. He breathed with difficulty. In a state of torpor, Dash Akol recognized Vali Khan. In a half-choked, trembling voice he said, "In the whole world… that parrot… was all I had… please… please… give it to…"

He fell silent again. Vali Khan took out his handkerchief and wiped the tears from his eyes. Dash Akol lost consciousness, and an hour later he died.

Everybody in Shiraz cried for him.

That afternoon, Marjan placed the parrot's cage in front of her and sat looking at the parrot's colourful wings, its hooked beak, and its round, lustreless eyes. Suddenly the parrot, in a rough, scratchy tone, said, "Marjan… Marjan… You killed me… Whom shall I tell… Marjan… Loving you… has destroyed me."

Tears streamed from Marjan's eyes.

The Man Who Killed His Passions

(from *Three Drops of Blood*)

> The passions are dragons,
> Perhaps sleeping, but never slain,
> In the proper circumstances,
> They'll rise up again.

Mowlavi*

REGULARLY EVERY MORNING, Mirza Hoseinali, wearing a black buttoned-up frock, pressed trousers, and shiny black shoes, came walking steadily out of one of the alleys near Sar Cheshme.* He passed in front of the Sepas-Selar Mosque, went through Safi Ali Shah Alley, and went to school.

He didn't look around as he walked. It was as if his thoughts were directed towards something special. He had a pure, dignified face, with small eyes, prominent lips and a brown moustache. His beard was always trimmed. He was very humble and quiet.

Occasionally around sunset, the thin figure of Mirza Hoseinali could be discerned from afar outside the city gate, walking very slowly, hands linked behind his back, head down, back bent. Sometimes he would stand and whisper to himself for a while, as if he were searching for something.

The principal of the school where he taught and the rest of the teachers neither liked nor disliked him. Perhaps he made a mysterious impression on them. In contrast to the teachers, the students were satisfied with him, because he had never been seen to be angry or to beat anybody. He was very calm and reserved, and he behaved in a pleasant manner towards the students. Because of this he was known for lacking authority, but in spite of that reputation, the students were polite in his class and were apprehensive of him. The only person with whom Mirza Hoseinali had a warm relationship and with whom he sometimes had discussions with was Sheikh Abelfazl, the teacher of Arabic, who was very pretentious. Sheikh Abelfazl was always talking about the degree to which he had mortified his flesh and the wondrous things he had done. For a long time he had been in a state of religious rapture, and he hadn't spoken for several years. He saw himself as a philosopher, heir to Avicenna, Mowlavi, and Galen. But in reality he was one of those selfish phoney mullahs who liked to show off his knowledge. In any conversation that arose he would immediately insert a proverb or an esoteric Arabic sentence, or he would cite a poem as evidence, and then with a victorious smile he would look for the effect of his words in the faces of those present. And it was strange that Mirza Hoseinali, the teacher of Persian and history, apparently modern and without pretension, should choose Sheikh Abelfazl of all people to be his friend. Sometimes he would take the Sheikh to his home, and sometimes he went to the Sheikh's house.

Mirza Hoseinali was from an old family, and was a knowledgeable, well-rounded man. People were impressed that he had graduated from the Darolfonoun. For two or three years he had travelled with his father on duty, but when he returned from the last trip he stayed in Tehran and chose the teaching profession, so that, even though he knew it was a difficult responsibility, he would have time to turn his attention to his own interest.

From childhood, from the time a mullah started to come to their house to tutor him and his brother, Mirza Hoseinali showed a special talent for learning the literature, poetry, and philosophy of the Sufis. He even wrote poetry in the Sufi style. Their teacher, Sheikh Abdollah, who considered himself a Sufi, paid special attention to his pupil. He indoctrinated him with mystic thoughts and described the mystic state for him. He had especially told him about the distinguished position of Mansour Hallaj, who by the mortification of his passions had elevated himself to such a position that even on the gallows he refused to stop saying "I am God". This story seemed very poetic to young Mirza Hoseinali. And finally one day Sheikh Abdollah declared to him, "With the nature that I see in you, if you follow the Way of Truth, you will attain excellence." Mirza Hoseinali always remembered this thought. It took root and grew in his brain, and he always wished for a suitable time to begin devoting himself to asceticism. Later he and his brother entered the Darolfonoun School.

There also, Mirza Hoseinali did very well in Arabic and literature. Mirza's younger brother was not of the same mind. He would mock him and say, "These fancies will only make you fall behind in life and give up your youth for nothing." But in his heart Mirza Hoseinali laughed at his brother's words; he considered his brother's thoughts materialistic and small, and he became even more stubborn in his determination. On account of this difference of opinion they separated after their father's death.

Something which reinforced Mirza's resolution was that on a recent trip to Kerjan he met a dervish* who, in the course of conversation, confirmed the words of his teacher, Sheikh Abdollah, and promised that if he should take up mysticism and discipline himself, he would reach a position of eminence. Thus it was that for five years Mirza Hoseinali had chosen seclusion and had closed the door to family and friends. He lived alone, and after his teaching, he would begin his main occupation at home.

His house was small and neat as a pin. He had an old housekeeper and an errand boy. As soon as he entered the door, he took his clothes off with care, hung them up, put on a long grey robe, and went into his library. He had allocated the largest room in the house for his library. At one corner beside the window a white mattress was spread. On it were two pillows. In front of it was a low table on which were several volumes, a pile of paper, a pen and an inkpot. The covers of the books on the table were worn. Many other books were stacked on shelves built into the wall.

The subject matter of these books was Gnosticism, mysticism, and ancient philosophy. His only recreation and pleasure was reading these books, and until midnight, behind the table under the oil lamp, he would pore over them and read. He would interpret them to himself and whatever seemed to him difficult or doubtful he would make a note of and later discuss with Sheikh Abelfazl. Not because Mirza Hoseinali was unable to understand their meaning: on the contrary, he had passed many of the spiritual stages and could penetrate hair-splitting ideas and the fine points of some Sufi poems better than Sheikh Abelfazl. He let these things inside, and he had created within himself a world beyond the material world. This had become a cause of egotism, because he considered himself to be superior to others, and he had complete faith in this superiority.

Mirza Hoseinali knew that there existed a secret in the world which the great Sufi had discovered, and it was evident to him that to begin the search he would need a preceptor, someone who would guide him. Sheikh Abdollah had told him, and he would read, that "because the initiate's thoughts are scattered at the beginning, he should concentrate on the teacher in order to collect his thoughts."

Thus it was that after searching a great deal he found Sheikh Abelfazl, even though he was not to Mirza's taste and knew nothing except for how to pass judgement. Whenever the Sheikh would encounter something difficult, he would say that it was too soon and he would explain it later, as if he were working with a child. In the end the only thing that Sheikh Abelfazl recommended to Mirza was to kill his passions. The Sheikh considered this the beginning of everything. In other words, by means of asceticism one could prevail over the senses, and the Sheikh delivered detailed lectures full of *hadith** which he had prepared about killing the passions. Among the things he said was: "Your worst enemy is inside you". Another was: "Your fight is with your passions". He quoted Chadi, who said: "Whoever kills his passions is a crusader". He also quoted the poem:

If the self can't be contained
It must somehow be restrained;
The fatal sword of ignorance
Should be sheathed in continence.

Another one he liked was:

To kill the passions should be our delight,
Man's highest honour is winning that fight.

Among other things which Sheikh Abolfazl preached there was this: "The seeker of the Truth should hold in contempt wealth, position, splendour, power and pomp, because the greatest wealth and pleasure is the subduing of the passions." He quoted Maktabi, who said:

Win the battle over self,
And attain eternal wealth.

And he said, "Know, oh friend of the Way, that if you are seduced once by the bodily senses, you have walked in the valley of death, just as Sanai says:

Keep your passions under control
If you would have them your slave.
Give them control and they will send
A thousand like you to the grave.

"And as Sheikh Saadi says:

If you help a man attain his ends
He'll help you achieve your desire.
The passions are different: foes, not friends.
Instead of helping, they'll rule you entire.

"And learned men of the Way have considered the passions as a vicious dog which must be bound by the chain of self-discipline and which one must avoid letting free. But the disciple must not become proud and reveal hidden secrets to the uninitiated. He should consult the preceptor at every difficulty. As Khawje Hāfiz, God bless him, says:

'This gallows was erected,' someone said,
'For giving secrets. Now the giver's dead.'"

Mirza Hoseinali had always had a special interest in asceticism and Indian philosophy, and he wished to go to India to pursue his studies. He wanted to meet members of Indian religious sects and learn their secrets. Thus he was not surprised by the suggestion that he should control his passions. On the contrary, he greeted it wholeheartedly, and the same day, when he returned home, he opened his handwritten copy of the *Masnvai** to find an omen. As luck would have it, these lines came up:

The passions do not keep their promises
For breaking faith they should be doomed to die.
The passions and their purpose both are base
And do their best themselves to justify.

In this society the passions fit
As aptly as the corpse fits in the grave.
The passions may be shrewd and full of wit
But to the temporal world they are as slaves.

Since in no afterlife do they have a part,
Leave them for dead. But God, who can't despise,
Can make his inspiration touch their heart –
From lifeless dust a being will arise.

This augury became the reason that Mirza Hoseinali decided definitely to spend all his effort in overcoming his natural instincts and devoting himself to asceticism. At first, the more profoundly he studied Sufi books, the more emphasis he put on this struggle. In the *Treatise of the True Light* it was written:

Oh master! Discipline yourself for some time
and occupy your passions in this endeavour,
until your false ideas leave and in their
place comes the truth.

In the *Conzelor Romus* of Mir Hoseini he read:

Destroy the passions, and their power break,
As you would destroy a vile snake.

In the book of Marsad ol'Bad it was written:

Know that when the initiate starts the struggle on the path of asceticism and the purification of the heart, the way to the kingdom of heaven appears to him; and at every stage secrets will unfold themselves to him befitting his state.

And in the poetry of Naser Khosro he read:

> There stands a dragon over your treasure,
> Slay it, and find sorrow turns to pleasure.
> To appease it, as the coward tries,
> Forfeits claim to that endless prize.

All of these threatening verses full of fear and hope, the writing of which had worn out countless pens, left little doubt in Mirza Hoseinali that the first step towards the goal was the killing of the devilish and animal passions, passions which prevented mankind from reaching the truth. Mirza Hoseinali wanted to purify his passion both through thought and reason and through rigour and struggle. Approximately a week of this passed, but then he began to be discouraged. The reason for this loss of hope was doubt and suspicion, especially after becoming involved with such poems as these by Hāfiz:

> Seek not the mystery of the universe,
> Rather tell tales of musicians and wine.
> For solving the riddle of our existence
> Requires a wisdom which no one can find.
> Enjoy each pleasant note that comes along,
> For no one knows the ending of life's song.

Although Mirza Hoseinali knew that words such as "wine", "cup-bearer", "tavern", "wine seller", and so on are mystical terminologies, still, in spite of this explanation, some of Khayyam's quatrains were very difficult for him and left him confused. For example:

> No one has seen Heaven and Hell, oh heart.
> From there none has returned, news to impart.
> Our hopes and fears are idle, for we have
> Nothing except the names from which to start.

Or this quatrain:

> Khayyam, if you are drunk with wine, rejoice,
> Happy with the beloved of your choice.

Because the end of life is nothingness,
Be glad that end has not yet stilled your voice.

These masters invited one to pleasure, whereas he had forbidden himself all pleasures. This thought produced a bitter regret in him for his past life – that life in which he had given up so much and which he had made so difficult for himself. Even now his days were painfully spent seeking imaginary ideas! For twelve years he had been giving himself sorrow and affliction. Of pleasure, of the happiness of youth, he had no share, and now, too, he was empty-handed. This doubt and hesitation had turned all his thoughts into frightening shadows which followed him everywhere. Especially at night, when he turned and twisted in the cold bed. Alone, no matter how much he wanted to think about spiritual worlds, as soon as he fell asleep and his thoughts grew dim, a hundred demons would tempt him. How many times did he leap awake in fright and pour cold water on his head and face? The next day he would eat less, and at night he would sleep on straw, because Sheikh Abelfazl was always reciting this poem for him:

The passions are like furies, hard to restrain,
The more they get, the louder they complain.

Mirza Hoseinali knew that if he slipped, all his efforts would be wasted. Because of this, he intensified the torturing and mortification of his body. But the more he disciplined himself, the more the demon of lust tortured him, until he decided to go to his only friend and teacher, Sheikh Abelfazl, relate his problems, and get complete instructions from him.

It was near dusk when this thought occurred to him. He changed his clothes, buttoned his frock, and with measured steps set out for the home of the teacher. When he arrived he saw a man standing angrily in front of the house. He was shouting and tearing his hair and saying aloud, "Tell the Sheikh tomorrow I'll take him to court, he'll have to answer me there. He took my daughter to be a maid and ruined her and took all her money. Either he has to marry her, or I'll tear him apart. I've been dishonoured…"

Mirza Hoseinali couldn't bear it any more. He went forwards and said softly, "My good man, you've made a mistake. This is the house of Sheikh Abelfazl."

"That's the same villain I'm talking to, that same godless sheikh. I know he's home, but he's hiding. If he had nerve enough to come out I'd tear him limb from limb. For sure I'll see him tomorrow."

When Mirza Hoseinali realized that the case was serious, he moved off and went away slowly, but these words were enough to awaken him. Could it be true? Hadn't he made a mistake? Sheikh Abelfazl, who had been recommending to him before anything else to kill the passions, hadn't he himself been able to succeed in this endeavour? Had he slipped, or had he been fooling Mirza? It was very important that he should know this. If it were true, then had all the Sufis been like this, saying things which they didn't believe themselves? Or was this typical only of his teacher, and had he found a phoney among the prophets? If this were the case, could he go and tell all his spiritual tortures and his misfortunes and then have the Sheikh recite several Arabic sentences, give him harder instructions, and laugh at him in his heart? No, he had to clear things up this very night. For a while he paced crazily about the empty streets. Then he found himself in a crowd. Without thinking of anything in particular, he walked slowly among the same people he had considered inferior and materialistic. Inside himself he felt their materialistic, ordinary life, and he desired to walk among them for a long while, but he turned once more towards Sheikh Abelfazl's house, as if he had made a sudden decision. This time no one else was there. He knocked on the door and told his name to the woman who answered it. It was a little while before she opened the door for him. When he entered the room he saw Sheikh Abelfazl, with his squinting eyes, pockmarked face, and beard dyed the colour of plum jam, sitting on a carpet. He was telling his beads and several volumes of books were open beside him. As he saw Mirza he sprang to his feet, said "Ya Allah" and cleared his throat. In front of him was an open handkerchief on which was some stale bread and an onion. The sheikh looked at Mirza and said, "Come in. Partake of a humble supper with a poor man for the evening."

"We thank you very much... Excuse me if I'm causing trouble. I was just passing by. I only came—"

"Not at all, nonsense. My house is yours."

Mirza Hoseinali wanted to say something, but suddenly there arose the sound of shouts and uproar, and a cat leapt into the room with a cooked partridge in its mouth and a yelling woman on its tail.

While Mirza Hoseinali watched, Sheikh Abelfazl suddenly threw his cloak at it, and wearing only a shirt and underpants, reached out and grabbed a club from the corner of the room and ran after the cat like a madman. Mirza Hoseinali forgot what he wanted to say and stood transfixed. After a quarter of an hour, panting and with a burning face, Sheikh Abelfazl entered the room and said, "You know, according to religious law, if a cat causes more than seven hundred dinars worth of damage it is a holy duty to kill it."

Mirza Hoseinali had no longer any doubt that this was a very ordinary man and that what the old man had charged was completely true. He got up and said, "Excuse me for bothering you... With your permission I'll leave."

Sheikh Abelfazl accompanied him to the door. When Mirza reached the alley he breathed a sigh of relief. Now it was proved for him. He recognized what kind of a man the Sheikh was and understood that this show and intrigue and trickery had been for his sake. He would eat a partridge, then, in order to fool people, he would set the table with dry bread and mouldy cheese or a withered onion to make himself seem pious. He instructed Mirza to eat nothing but an almond a day, while he himself got the maid pregnant and recited with relish this poem of Attar's:

> Don't shed blood, like the wild beast, oh son,
> That unbefitting food try hard to shun.
> Be happy with a morsel or a grain,
> Through fasting keep your passions bound in chains.
> In fasting strive for excellence, and find
> You'll achieve distinction from your kind.
> Don't merely keep food from the passions hidden,
> But refuse all thoughts on things forbidden.

It was dark. Once more Mirza Hoseinali entered the crowd of people. Like a lost child he walked aimlessly in the dusty, crowded streets. In the light of the streetlamps he looked at faces. All of them were dull and sad. His head felt empty, and there was a pressure in his heart which had grown unbearable. These people whom he had considered base, bound to their stomachs and lusts, gathering money, he now knew to be wiser and better than he, and he wished to be one of them. But he said to himself, "Who knows?" Maybe there was someone among them even worse off than he. Could he judge from appearances? Wouldn't a beggar on the street become happier with just one coin than the richest person? While all the money in the world couldn't do anything to alleviate Mirza Hoseinali's pain. This time all the frightening nightmares which usually came to him were stronger and quicker in their attack. It occurred to him that his life had passed uselessly. Frenzied, confused memories of thirty years passed before him. He felt himself to be the most unfortunate and useless of creatures. Periods of his life appeared to him from behind dark clouds. Some episodes would shine out suddenly, then they would disappear. All of it was monotonous, tiring, and heart-rending. Sometimes a brief, vain happiness appeared like lightning flashing from a cloud. Everything seemed mean and useless to him: what a worthless struggle! What an absurd chase! He muttered to himself and bit his lips. His youth had been wasted in seclusion and darkness, without pleasure, without happiness, without love, weary of himself and others. How many people sometimes feel themselves more lost, more homeless than a bird which cries in the darkness of the night? He could no longer believe anything. This meeting of his with Sheikh Abelfazl had cost him dearly, because it had turned all his thoughts inside out. He was tired and thirsty, and a devil or a dragon had awakened in him which continually wounded and poisoned him. Now a car passed him, and in its lights his angry face, trembling lips and open, expressionless eyes were frighteningly illuminated. He was gazing into space, with a half open mouth, as if he were laughing at something out of reach. He felt a pressure at the base of his skull which extended to his forehead and temples and caused wrinkles to appear between his eyebrows.

Mirza Hoseinali had felt pain beyond human endurance. He was acquainted with hopeless hours, with distress and misfortune, and he knew a kind of philosophical pain which doesn't exist for the mass of people. But now he felt himself immeasurably lost and alone. Life for him had become nothing but a mockery and a lie. He recited to himself, "What do I have to show for life? Nothing!"

This line from a poem drove him mad. Pale moonlight shone from behind the clouds, but he passed in the shadows. This moon, which previously had been so enchanting and mysterious for him and with whom he had communed during long hours outside the city gate, now seemed a cold, heartless and meaningless brightness. It angered him. He remembered the warm days, the long hours of study. He remembered his youth. While other boys his age were busy with pleasure, he would spend the summer days dripping with sweat, studying Arabic grammar with other students. Then they would go to take part in discussions with their theology teacher, Sheikh Mohammad Taqi. Squatting in full gathered trousers, a bowl of ice water in front of him, he fanned himself, and if they made a mistake in one vowel sign of an Arabic word, he shouted and the veins of his neck stood out, as if the world were ending.

Now the streets were empty and the shops were closed. When he entered Allah-o-Duleh Street the sound of music aroused him. Over a blue door in the glow of an electric light he read the name "Maxim". Without hesitating he pushed back the curtain in the doorway, entered, and sat down at a table.

Since Mirza Hoseinali wasn't used to bars, having never set foot inside such places, he looked around in amazement. Cigarette smoke mingled with the smell of fried meat and cabbage. A short man with a heavy moustache and rolled-up sleeves stood behind the bar working out sums on an abacus. A row of bottles was arranged next to him. A bit further away, a fat woman was playing the piano, while a thin man beside her played the violin. Drunken customers with strange faces, some from Russia and the Caucasus, sat at the tables. Meanwhile, a rather pretty woman with a foreign accent came up to his table and said with a smile, "Won't you buy me a glass of wine, darling?"

"Certainly."

Without hesitation the woman called a waiter and ordered an alcoholic drink he had never heard of. The waiter placed a bottle of wine and two glasses in front of them. The woman poured the wine and offered it to him. Mirza Hoseinali reluctantly drank the first glass. His body grew warm, his thoughts mixed up. The woman plied him with glass after glass of alcohol. A mournful wailing came from the violin. Mirza Hoseinali felt free and peculiarly happy inside. He remembered all the praise and glorification of wine he had read in Sufi poetry. In the pitiless brightness of the light he saw crow's feet around the eyes of the woman seated next to him. After all his self-restraint, now his lot had become a yellow, sour-tasting wine and a heavily made-up, used, rough-haired woman. But he liked it that way. He felt he wanted to lower himself so that he could better destroy and ruin the being he had become through so much pain. He wanted to plunge from the purest, brightest thoughts into the darkest pleasure. He wanted to become a laughing stock, have people jeer at him. He wanted to find a route of escape for himself through madness. In this hour he knew himself capable of every kind of insanity. He murmured to himself:

> During this time of poverty
> Have pleasure, feast, and revelry
> The philosopher's stone of existence
> Can turn a beggar to a Croesus.

Opposite him, the Russian woman laughed. Everything Mirza Hoseinali had read in Sufi poetry in praise of wine appeared before his eyes. He felt it all; he could read all the mysteries and secrets in the face of the woman who was sitting opposite him. At this time he was happy, because he had attained what he had wished for. Through the delicate mist of the wine he saw what he could never have imagined, what Sheikh Abelfazl couldn't even dream, what other people couldn't even conceive. Another world, full of secrets, became apparent to him. He understood that those who had forbidden this world had taken all their words and comparisons and allusions from it.

When Mirza Hoseinali got up to pay the bill he couldn't stand on his feet. He took out his wallet, gave it to the woman, and with his arm around her they went out of Maxim's. In the droshky, Mirza Hoseinali laid his head on the woman's breast. He breathed the smell of her powder. The world was whirling before his eyes. The lights were dancing. The woman sang a mournful song in her Russian accent.

The droshky stopped at Mirza Hoseinali's house. He entered the house with the woman, but he didn't go to the bed of straw where he usually slept. He took her to the white mattress which was spread in his library.

Two days passed, and Mirza Hoseinali didn't go to his work at school. On the third day was written in the newspaper: "Mister Mirza Hoseinali, a young, hardworking teacher, has committed suicide for unknown reasons."

Buried Alive

(from *Buried Alive*)

I'M SHORT OF BREATH, tears pour from my eyes, my mouth tastes sour. I'm dizzy, my heartbeat is laboured, I'm exhausted, beaten, my body is loosened up. I have fallen without volition on the bed. My arms are punctured from injections. My bed smells of sweat and fever. I look at the clock on the small table beside the bed. It's Sunday, ten o'clock. I look at the ceiling of the room, from the middle of which hangs a light bulb. I look around the room. The wallpaper has a pink and red flower design. At intervals two blackbirds sit opposite each other on a branch. One of them has opened his beak as if he is talking to the other. This picture infuriates me, I don't know why, but whichever direction I turn, it's before my eyes. The table is covered with bottles, wicks, and boxes of medicine. The smell of burnt alcohol, the smell of a sickroom, has pervaded the air. I want to get up and open the window, but an over-whelming laziness has nailed me to the bed. I want to smoke a cigarette, but I have no desire for it. It hasn't been ten minutes since I shaved my beard, which had grown long. I came and fell in bed. When I looked in the mirror I saw that I'd become very wasted and thin. I walked with difficulty. The room is a mess. I'm alone.

A thousand kinds of astonishing thoughts whirl and circle in my brain. I see all of them. But to write the smallest feeling or the least passing idea I must describe my whole life, and that isn't possible. These reflections, these feelings, are the result of my whole life, the result of my way of life, of my inherited thoughts, of what I've seen, heard, read, felt, or pondered over. All these things have made up my irrational and ridiculous existence.

I twist in the bed. I jumble my memories together. Distressed and mad reflections press my brain. My head hurts, throbs. My temples are hot. I twist and turn. I pull the quilt over my eyes. I think – I'm tired. It would be good if I could open my head and take out all the soft, grey, twisted mass of my brain and throw it all away, throw it to a dog.

Nobody can understand. Nobody will believe. To somebody who fails at everything they say, "Go and lay your head down and die." But when even death doesn't want you, when even death turns its back on you, death which won't come and which doesn't want to come!..."

Everyone is afraid of death but I'm afraid of my persistent life. How frightening it is when death doesn't want one and rejects one! Only one thing consoles me. It was two weeks ago, I read in the paper that in Austria a person tried thirteen times to kill himself in different ways and each time he almost succeeded: he hanged himself and the rope broke, he threw himself in the river and they pulled him out, and so on... Finally, for the last time, when the house was empty he slashed his wrists with a kitchen knife, and this thirteenth time he died!

This gives me consolation!

No, no one decides to commit suicide. Suicide is with some people. It is in their very nature, they can't escape it. It is fate which rules, but at the same time it is I who have created my own fate. Now I can no longer escape it, but I cannot escape from myself.

Anyhow, what can be done? Fate is stronger than I am. What fancies I get! As I was lying in bed I wished to be a child. The same old nursemaid who used to tell me stories, pausing to swallow, would be sitting here at my head. I would be lying just like this, tired out in bed, and she would elaborately tell me stories and my eyes would slowly close. Now that I think about it, some of the events of my childhood come easily to mind. It is as if it were yesterday. I see that I'm not very far from my childhood. Now I see the whole of my dark, base, and useless life. Was I happy then? No, what a big mistake! Everyone supposes children are lucky. No, how well I remember. I was even more sensitive then. Then I was a phoney and a sly fellow. On the surface I may have laughed or played, but inside, the least biting remark or the smallest unpleasant, worthless occurrence, would occupy my mind for long hours, and I would eat my heart out. By no means should a character like mine survive. The truth is with those who say that heaven and hell are inside a person. Some are born lucky and some unlucky.

I look at the red pencil stub with which I am making these notes in bed. It was with the same pencil that I wrote out the meeting place and the note to the girl whom I had just got to know. We went to the pictures

were nightmares. I was neither asleep nor awake, but I saw them. My body was enervated, beaten, sick and heavy. My head hurt. These frightening nightmares kept passing before my eyes. Sweat dripped from my body. I saw a package of paper opening in the air. It dropped sheet by sheet. A group of soldiers passed, their faces invisible. The dark, terrifying night was filled with frightening and angry figures. When I wanted to close my eyes and give myself up to death, these startling images would appear. A volcanic circle whirling about itself, a corpse floating on a river, eyes looking at me from every direction. Now I remember well the crazy, angry figures swarming towards me. An old man with a bloody face had been tied to a column. He was looking at me, laughing; his teeth glittered. A bat was hitting my face with its cold wings. I was walking on a tightrope. Below it was a whirlpool. I was slipping. I wanted to scream. A hand was laid on my shoulder. An icy hand was pressing my throat. It seemed that my heart would stop. The groans, the sinister groans which came from the night's darkness, the faces cleaned of shadows – these things appeared and disappeared of their own accord. What could I do in the face of them? They were at once very near and very far. I wasn't dreaming them because I hadn't yet fallen asleep.

* * *

I don't know if I have fooled everyone or if I have been fooled, but there is one thought which is driving me crazy. I can't stop myself from laughing. Sometimes I choke with laughter. So far nobody has understood what's wrong with me. They've all been fooled! It's been a week that I've been pretending to be sick, or else I've caught a strange ailment. Willy-nilly I picked up a cigarette and lit it. Why do I smoke? I don't know myself. I hold the cigarette between two fingers of my left hand. I lift it to my lips. I blow the smoke into the air. This is also an ailment!

Now when I think about it my body trembles. It's no joke – for a week I tortured myself in various ways. I wanted to become ill. The weather had been cold for several days. First I went and turned the cold water on myself. I left the bathroom windows open. Now when I think of it, I get the creeps. I was gasping, my back and chest hurt, I told myself that now everything was over. The next day my chest would hurt badly, and I would be confined to bed. I would make it worse and then put an end to myself. The next morning when I woke up I didn't find the smallest sign of a cold. Again I took off my clothes. When it got dark I locked the door, turned off the light, opened the window and sat in the stinging cold. A sharp wind was blowing. I trembled violently. I could hear my teeth chattering. I looked outside. The people who were coming and going, their black shadows, the cars which were passing, all appeared small from the sixth floor of the building. I had surrendered my naked body to the cold, and I was writhing. At this point it occurred to me that I was crazy. I laughed at myself. I laughed at life. I knew that in this big playhouse of the world everybody plays in a certain way until his death arrives. I had taken up this role because I thought I would be carried off the stage sooner. My lips were dry. The cold burned my body. I warmed myself until I dripped with sweat, then all at once I stripped. All night I lay on the bed and trembled. I didn't sleep at all. I got a mild cold, but as soon as I took a nap the illness completely went away. I saw this didn't help either. For three days I didn't eat anything, and every night I stripped and sat in front of the window. I would make myself tired. One night until morning I ran on an empty stomach through the streets of Paris. I got tired and went and sat on the cold damp steps in a narrow alley. It was past midnight. A drunken worker reeled by. In the vague mysterious gaslight I saw a man and a woman passing and talking together. Then I got up and started to walk. Homeless wretches were sleeping on the street benches.

Finally I took to bed from weakness, but I wasn't sick. My friends came to see me. I made myself tremble in front of them, and I acted sick so well that they were sorry for me. They thought I would die the next day. I said my heartbeat was laboured. When they left the room I mocked them. I said to myself that there seemed to be only one thing in the world I could do well. I should have become an actor!…

How did I pull off the same trick on the doctors that I did on my friends? Everyone believed that I was truly sick. Whatever they asked, I said, "My heartbeat is laboured", because sudden death can only be attributed to a heart attack; otherwise, a simple chest pain could hardly be fatal.

This was a miracle. When I think of it, a strange feeling comes over me. I had been torturing myself for seven days. If, at the insistence of my friends, I had a cup of tea, I'd get better. It was frightening. The illness would completely go away. How badly I wanted to eat the bread alongside the tea, but I didn't do it. Every night I would say to myself that finally I had become bedridden. Tomorrow I wouldn't be able to get up. I went and brought the capsules that I had filled with opium. I put them in the drawer of the small table beside my bed so that when the illness had really thrown me and I couldn't move, I could bring them out and swallow them. Unfortunately the illness wouldn't come and didn't want to come. Once when I was obliged to eat a piece of bread with tea in front of one of my friends, I felt that I was well, all well. I became scared of myself, my own endurance frightened me. It's terrifying. It's unbelievable. I am in my right mind as I write this. I'm not speaking nonsense. I remember well.

What was this strength that had appeared in me? I saw that none of my plans had worked. I really had to become ill. Yes, the fatal poison is there in my bag, a swift poison. I remembered the rainy day that I bought it with lies and pretexts and a thousand difficulties, pretending to be a photographer. I gave a false name and address. Potassium cyanide, which I had read about in a medical book and whose signs I knew: convulsion, difficulty in breathing, agony when taken on an empty stomach. Twenty grams of it kills immediately or within two minutes. So that it wouldn't spoil in the air I had wrapped it in a chocolate wrapper, covered this with a layer of wax, and put it in a crystal bottle with a stopper. It was a hundred grams, and I kept it with me like a precious jewel. But fortunately I found something better than that – smuggled opium, and that in Paris! The opium which I had been after for such a long time, I found by accident. I had read that dying by taking opium is better and more wholesome than doing so by cyanide. Now I wanted to make myself really sick and then take the opium.

I unwrapped the potassium cyanide. I shaved off about two grams from the egg shaped ball and put it in an empty capsule: I sealed it with glue and swallowed it. Half an hour passed. I felt nothing. The surface of the capsule, which had touched the poison, tasted salty. I took out the cyanide again. This time I shaved off about five grams and swallowed the capsule. I went and lay down on the bed. I lay down as if I would never get up again!

This thought could drive anyone mad. No, I didn't feel anything. The killer poison didn't work on me! I'm still alive, and the poison is lying there in my bag. In the bed my breath comes with difficulty, but that's not the result of the drug. I have become invincible, invincible like those in legends. It's unbelievable, but I must go. It's futile. I feel rejected, useless, good for nothing. I should end things as soon as possible and go. This time it's not a joke. The more I think the more I see that nothing holds me to life, nothing and no one...

I remember it was the day before yesterday. I was pacing my room like a madman, going from one side to the other. The clothes hanging from the wall, the sink, the mirror in the cupboard, the picture on the wall, the bed, the table in the middle of the room, the books scattered on it, the chairs, the shoes placed under the cupboard, the suitcases in a corner of the room, passed continually before my eyes. But I wasn't seeing them, or else I wasn't concentrating. What was I thinking of? I don't know – I was pacing around to no purpose. Suddenly I came to myself. I had seen this frenzied pacing somewhere else and it had attracted my attention. I didn't know where, then I remembered. It was in the Berlin zoo that I had seen wild animals for the first time. Those that were awake in their cages walked in this same way, just like this. I too had become like those animals. Perhaps I even thought as they did. Inside I felt that I was like them. This mechanical walking around in a circle. When I bumped into the wall I naturally felt that it was a barrier, and turned around. Those animals do the same thing...

I don't know what I'm writing. The clock goes tick-tock right in my ear. I want to pick it up and throw it out of the window. This frightening sound that beats the passing of time into my head with a hammer!

For a week I had been making myself ready for death. I destroyed all the papers and things I had written. I threw away my dirty clothes so that when my things were being investigated nothing dirty would be found. I put on the new underwear I had bought, so that when they pulled me out of bed and the doctor came to examine me I would look presentable. I picked up a bottle of eau de cologne and sprinkled in the bed so it would smell good. But since none of my actions was like those of other people, I wasn't sure this time either. I was afraid of my die-hard self. It was as if this distinction and superiority aren't given to one easily. I knew that nobody dies for free...

I took out the pictures of my relatives and looked at them. Each one of them appeared before me reflecting my own observations of them. I liked them and I didn't like them. I wanted to see them and I didn't want to. No, those memories were too bright before my eyes. I tore up the pictures; I was not attached to anything. I judged myself and saw I had not been a kind person. I had been created hard, rough, and weary. Maybe I wasn't always like this, but life and the passage of time have made me so. I have no fear of death. On the contrary, an illness, a special madness had appeared in me so that I was drawn by the magnetism of death. This isn't recent, either. I remembered a story from five or six years ago. In Tehran one early morning I went to Shah Abad Avenue to buy opium from a druggist. I put three tomans in front of him and said, "Two rials of opium."

Wearing a henna-dyed beard and a skullcap on his head and uttering holy words, he looked at me shrewdly, as if he were a physiognomist or could read my thoughts and said, "We don't have change."

I took out a two-rial coin to give him. He said, "No, we don't sell it at all." I asked why and he said, "You're young and ignorant. You might suddenly decide to eat the opium, God forbid." I didn't insist.

No, no one decides to commit suicide. Suicide is with some people. It's in their very nature. Yes, everyone's fate is written on his forehead; some people are born with suicide. I always mocked life, the world and its peoples all seemed like a game, a humiliation, something empty and meaningless. I wanted to sleep a dreamless sleep and not wake up again. But since people see suicide as a strange thing, I wanted to make myself ill, to become worn out and weak, and when everyone thought I was really sick, to eat the opium, so that people would say, "He fell ill and died."

* * *

I am writing in bed. It's three in the afternoon. Two people came to see me. They just left. I'm alone. My head is spinning, my body is comfortable and calm. There's a cup of milk and tea in my stomach. My body is loose, feeble, and feverish. I remembered a pretty tune I heard once on a record. I want to whistle it but I can't. I wished I could hear that record again. Right now I neither like life nor dislike it. I am alive but without will or desire; a superior power is holding me. I have been bound in the prison of life with steel chains. If I were dead they would take me to the Paris mosque. I would fall into the hands of those damn Arabs and I would die again. I am sick and tired of them. In any case it wouldn't make any difference to me. If they threw me into a sewer after I died it would be the same for me, I would rest easy. Only my family would cry and weep. They would bring my picture, praise me, all of the usual rot. All of this seems foolish and futile to me. Probably a few people would praise me, a few would criticize, but finally I would be forgotten. I am basically selfish and without charm.

The more I think about it the more I see that continuing this life is futile. I am a germ in the body of society, a harmful being, a burden on others. Sometimes my madness breaks out again. I want to go away, far away, to a place where I could forget myself, to go very far, for example go to Siberia, in wooden houses, under pine trees, with grey skies, snow, lots of snow, among the Mujiks, go and start my life over again. Or, for example, go to India, under the shining sun, in the dense forests, among strange people; go somewhere where no one knows me, nobody knows my language. I want to feel everything within myself. But I see I wasn't made for this. No, I'm lazy and good for nothing. I was born by mistake. I'm untouchable, driven from pillar to post. I have closed my eyes to all my plans, to love, to delight. I put everything aside. From now on I may be considered among the dead.

Sometimes I make big plans, I see myself worthy of every job and every thing. I say to myself, "Yes, only people who have washed their hands of life and have been disappointed in everything can accomplish great things." Then I say to myself, "What's the use? What purpose would it serve? Madness, everything is madness. No, do away with yourself, and leave your corpse to rot. Get lost, you weren't made for life. Leave off being philosophical, your existence has no value, you can't do anything." But I don't know why death was coy. Why didn't it come? Why couldn't I succeed with my plan and become comfortable? I had tortured myself for a week and this was the return I got! Poison didn't affect me. It's unbelievable; I can't believe it. I didn't eat, I tried to get pneumonia, I drank vinegar. Every night I thought I had come down with a severe case of tuberculosis, but in the morning when I got up my health was better than the day before. Who can I tell this to? I didn't even get a fever. But I haven't dreamt, nor have I taken narcotics. I remember everything well. No, it's unbelievable.

Now that I've written this down I am feeling a little better. It consoles me. It's as if a heavy burden has been lifted from my shoulders. How good it would be if everything could be written. If I could have made others understand my thoughts I would. No, there are feelings, there are things, which can't be conveyed to others, which can't be told, people would mock you. Everybody judges other people on the basis of his own values. Language, like man himself, is imperfect and incapable.

I'm invincible. Poison didn't affect me. I ate opium to no effect. Yes, I've become invincible. No other poison will affect me. Finally I realized that all my life was wasted. It was the night before last – I decided that before this mockery started to arouse suspicion, I would end it. I went and took out the capsules of opium from the drawer of the small table. There were three, approximately the size of an ordinary stick of opium all together. I picked them up. It was seven o'clock. I asked for tea from downstairs. They brought it and I drank it down. By eight, no one had come to see me. I closed the door from inside. I went and stood in front of the picture that was on the wall. I looked at it. I don't know what occurred to me, but in my eyes he was a stranger. I said to myself, "What relationship does this person have with me?" But I know that face. I had seen it a lot. Then I came back. I felt neither frenzy, nor fear, nor happiness. All the things I had done and the things I wanted to do and everything seemed to me to be useless and empty. Life seemed completely ridiculous. I looked around the room. Everything was in its place. I went in front of the cupboard mirror and looked at my flushed face. I half closed my eyes, opened my mouth a little bit and held my head bent like a dead man's. I said to myself, "Tomorrow morning I'll look like this. First, no matter how much they knock no one will answer. Till noon they'll think I'm sleeping. Then they'll break the lock, enter the room, and see me like this." All of these thoughts passed like lightning through my mind. I picked up a glass of water. Coolly I told myself it was an aspirin, and swallowed the first capsule. The second and third also I swallowed hastily one after another. I felt a slight trembling inside me. My mouth smelled like opium. My heart beat a little faster. I threw the half-smoked cigarette in the ashtray. I took a scented wafer from my pocket and sucked it. I looked at myself once more in the mirror. I looked around the room – everything was in its place. I told myself that now everything was over. Tomorrow even Plato couldn't bring me back to life. I straightened the clothes on the chair by the bed. I pulled the quilt over myself. It had absorbed the smell of eau de cologne. I switched off the light and the room darkened. Part of the wall and the foot of the bed were slightly lit by the weak glow that came from the window. I had nothing else to do. Good or bad, I had brought things to this point. I lay down. I turned. I was fearful that someone might come to see how I was and be insistent. However, I had told everyone that I hadn't been able to sleep for several nights, so that they would leave me alone. I was very curious at that time, as if an important event had taken place or I was going to go on an exciting trip. I wanted to feel death well. I had concentrated my senses, yet I was listening for sounds outside. As soon as a footstep came, my heart would cave in. I pressed my eyelids together. Ten minutes or so went by. Nothing happened. I had occupied myself with different thoughts till I felt the pills begin to work, but I didn't regret this decision of mine, nor was I afraid. First I became heavy. I felt tired. This feeling was more in the pit of my stomach, like when food isn't well digested. Then this feeling travelled to my chest and then to my head. I moved my hands. I became thirsty. My mouth had turned dry. I swallowed with difficulty. My heartbeat slowed. A short time passed. I felt that warm, pleasant air was being given off from my body, more from the extremities like the fingertips, the tip of the nose, and so on... At the same time I knew that I wanted to kill myself. I realized that this news would be unpleasant for some people. Everything seemed amazing. All of this seemed childish, absurd, and laughable to me. I thought to myself that now I was comfortable and I would die easily. What did it matter whether others would be sad or not, would cry or not? I greatly desired that this should happen and I feared lest I should move or think in such a way that I would prevent the opium from working. My only fear was that after all this trouble I might remain alive. I feared that dying might be difficult and that in despair I might cry out or want someone to help me. But I said that no matter how hard it was, opium puts one to sleep and he feels nothing. Sleep – I would sleep and I wouldn't be able to move from my place or say anything, and the door was locked from inside!...

Yes, I remember well. These thoughts came to me. I heard the monotonous sound of the clock. I heard the footsteps of people who were walking in the guesthouse. It seemed as if my sense of hearing had become sharper. I felt that my body was flying. My mouth had become dry. I had a slight headache. I had almost fallen into a faint. My eyes were half open. My breathing was sometimes fast, sometimes slow. From all the pores of my skin this pleasant heat flowed out of my body. It was as if I too were going out after it. I really wanted its intensity to increase. I had plunged into an unspeakable ecstasy. I thought whatever I wanted to. If I moved I felt that it would be a hindrance to the flowing out of this warmth. The more comfortably I lay the better it was. I pulled my right hand out from under me. I rolled over and lay on my back. It was somewhat unpleasant. I returned to the first position, and the effect of the opium became stronger. I wanted to feel death fully. My feelings had grown strong and magnified. I was amazed that I didn't fall asleep. It was as if all of my existence was leaving my body happily and wholesomely. My heart beat slowly. I breathed slowly. I think two or three hours passed. At this point someone knocked on the door. I realized it was my neighbour, but I didn't answer him and I didn't want to move from my place. I opened my eyes and closed them again. I heard the sound of his door opening. He washed his hands and whistled to himself. I heard everything. I tried to think happy, pleasant thoughts. I was thinking of the past year. The day when I was sitting in the boat and they were playing instruments. The waves of the sea, the rocking of the boat, the pretty girl sitting opposite me: I had plunged into my thoughts. I was running after them, as if I had wings and was soaring through space. I had grown so light and nimble that it can't be explained. The difference of being under the pleasurable influence of opium is as great as the difference between light seen ordinarily or seen through a chandelier or a crystal prism which separates it into different colours. In this state any simple, empty thoughts which come to people become enchanting and dazzling of themselves. Any passing and empty thought appears entrancing and splendid. If a scene or a vista passes through one's mind, it becomes limitlessly large, space swells, the passing of time is imperceptible.

At this time I felt very happy. My senses undulated above me. But I felt that I wasn't asleep. The last feeling that I remember of the pleasure and ecstasy of the opium is that my legs had become cold and senseless, my body motionless. I felt that I was going, drifting far away. But as soon as its influence waned, an infinite sorrow gripped me. I felt that my senses were returning. It was very difficult and unpleasant. I was cold. For more than half an hour I trembled violently. I could hear my teeth chattering. Then came fever, burning fever, and sweat poured from my body. My heart laboured, my breathing had become difficult. The first thought that occurred to me was that all my work was undone, and things hadn't turned out as they should have. I was surprised at my useless endurance. I realized that a dark power and an unspeakable misfortune were fighting me.

With difficulty I sat up partly in the bed. I pressed the light switch. It became light. I don't know why my hand went towards the small mirror that was on the bedside table. I saw that my face had swollen and had a sallow colouring. Tears fell from my eyes. My heart struggled hard. I told myself that at least my heart was ruined. I turned off the light and fell back in the bed.

No, my heart wasn't ruined. Today it's better. A bad product has no buyers. The doctor came to see me. He listened to my heart, took my pulse, looked at my tongue, took my temperature, the same things that doctors do everywhere, as soon as they see a patient. He gave me a mixture of baking powder and quinine. He didn't understand at all what my pain was! No one can understand my pain! These medicines are laughable. There in rows on the table are seven or eight kinds of medicine. I was laughing to myself. What a theatre this is.

The clock ticks incessantly by my ear. From outside come the sounds of car and bicycle horns, the clang of trains. I look at the wallpaper, the deep purple leaves and white flowers. At intervals on the branches two blackbirds are seated facing one another. My head is empty, my stomach twisting, my body broken. The newspapers which I have thrown on top of the cabinet lie there in odd positions. When I look it suddenly seems as if everything is strange to me. I even seem a stranger to myself. I wonder why I'm still alive. Why do I breathe? Why do I get hungry? Why do I eat? Why do I walk? Why am I here? Who are these people that I see, and what do they want from me?...

Now I know myself well, just the way I am, no more, no less. I can't do anything. I have fallen on the bed tired and exhausted. My thoughts revolve, whirl, hour by hour. I have become bored in their hopeless circle. My own existence astonishes me. How bitter and frightening it is when someone feels his own existence! When I look in the mirror I laugh at myself. To me my face seems so unknown and strange and laughable...

This thought has occurred to me many times: I've become invulnerable. The invincibility that has been described in legends is my tale. It was a miracle. Now I believe all kinds of superstitions and rubbish. Amazing thoughts pass before my eyes. It was a miracle. Now I know that in his endless cruelty, God or some other snake in the grass created two kinds of beings: the fortunate and the unfortunate. He supports the first group, while making the second group increase their torture and oppression by their own hands. Now I believe that a mean, brutal force, an angel of misfortune, is with some people.

* * *

Finally I've been left alone. The doctor left just now. I've picked up paper and pencil. I want to write. I don't know what. Either I have nothing to write or I can't write because there's so much. This itself is a misfortune. I don't know. I can't cry. Maybe if I could it would soothe me a little bit! I can't. I look like a lunatic. I saw in the mirror that my hair is a mess. My eyes are open and empty. I think my face shouldn't have looked like this at all. Many people's faces don't go with their thoughts. This really irritates me. All I know is that I hate myself. I eat and hate myself, walk and hate myself, think and hate myself. How obstinate. How frightening! No, this was a supernatural power, a loathsome disease. Now I believe these kind of things. Nothing will affect me any more. I took cyanide and it had no effect on me, I ate opium and I'm still alive! If a dragon bites me, the dragon will die! No, no one would believe it. Had these poisons spoilt? Wasn't the amount sufficient? Was it more than the normal dose? Had I mistaken the amount when I looked in the medical book? Or does my hand turn the poison into antidote? I don't know. These thoughts have come to me hundreds of times. There's nothing new in them. I remember I have heard that when a scorpion is surrounded by a ring of fire it stings itself – isn't there a ring of fire around me?

Outside my window on the black edge of the tin roof, where rainwater has collected, two sparrows are sitting. One of them puts its beak into the water, then lifts its head. The other one, crouching next to it, is pecking at itself. I just moved. Both of them chirped and flew off together. The weather is cloudy. Sometimes the pale sun appears behind a bit of cloud. The tall buildings opposite are all covered with soot, black and sad under the pressure of this heavy, rainy weather. The distant, suffocated sound of the city can be heard.

There in the drawer of my table are the malicious cards with which I told my fortune, those lying cards which fooled me. The funniest thing is that I still tell my fortune with them!

What can be done? Fate is stronger than I am.

It would be good if, with the experience of life that a person has, he could be born again and start his life anew. But which life? Is it in my hands? What's the use? A blind and frightening force rules us. There are people whose fate is directed by a sinister star. They break under this burden, and they want to be broken...

I have neither wishes nor grudges left. I have lost whatever in me was human. I let it be lost. In life one must become either an angel, a human being, or an animal. I became none of these. My life was lost forever. I was born selfish, clumsy, and miserable. Now, it is impossible for me to go back and adopt another way. I can't follow these useless shadows any more, grappling with life, what firm reason and logic do you have? I no longer want to pardon or to be pardoned, to go to the left or to the right. I want to close my eyes to the future and forget the past.

No, I can't flee from my fate. Aren't they the truth, these crazy thoughts, these feelings, these passing fancies which come to me? In any case they seem more natural and less artificial than my logical thoughts. I suppose I am free, yet I can't resist my fate. My reins are in the hands of my fate, fate is what pulls me from one side to another. The meanness, the baseness of life, which can't be fought against. Stupid life.

Now I am neither living nor sleeping. Nothing pleases me and nothing bothers me. I have become acquainted with death, used to it. It is my only friend. It is the only thing which heartens me. I remember the Montparnasse Cemetery. I don't envy the dead anymore. I am now counted in their world. I, too, am with them. I am buried alive...

I'm tired. What trash have I written? I say to myself, "Go, lunatic, throw away the paper and the pencil, throw them away. That's enough rambling. Shut up. Tear it up, lest this rubbish fall into somebody's hands. How would they judge me? But I wouldn't be embarrassed, nothing is important to me. I laugh at the world and whatever is in it. However harsh their judgement of me might be, they don't know that I have already judged myself even harder. They'll laugh at me; they don't know that I laugh at them more. I am sick of myself and of everyone who reads this trash.

These notes and a pack of cards were in his drawer. He himself was lying in bed. He had forgotten to breathe.

Paris, Esfand 11, 1308
(3rd March 1928)

Notes

p. 3, *Karbala*: A city in Iraq, one of the Muslim holy cities to which pilgrimages are made.

p. 12, *Darolfonoun*: The name of a school in Tehran

p. 19, *Pass Qale*: A village north of Tehran

p. 20, *Aide Qorban*: A day of sacrifice in the Muslim religion.

p. 25, *I divorced my wife three times*: According to Islamic law a divorce comes into effect when the husband tells the wife, "I divorce you". At this point the couple can remarry if they wish. However, if the husband tells the wife "I divorce you, I divorce you, I divorce you", then they cannot remarry unless the wife marries someone else first and is divorced from him. This person is called a legalizer.

p. 29, *the Shah Abdolazim cemetery*: A cemetery in southern Tehran containing the tomb of Shah Abdolazim, a holy figure.

p. 32, *Pah Chenar*: A village outside of Tehran

p. 33, *thirteenth day of Mehr 1311*: The date given refers to the Muslim solar calendar. 1311 A.H. corresponds to 1932 AD.

p. 34, *Bandargaz*: An Iranian port on the Caspian Sea.

p. 41, *Flandon*: Hedayat says "E. Flandon and P. Coste were two well-known Iranologists, who ninety years ago did important research about ancient Iran. This section has been taken from Flandon's notes." They published *Voyage on Perse* in 1851.

p. 46, *Muharri and Safar*: Months of mourning for the deaths of holy figures in the Shi'a branch of the Muslim religion

p. 46, *the passion plays*: Plays re-enacting the martyrdoms of Muslim religious figures.

p. 77, *Imam*: A title given to certain religious leaders in the Muslim religion.

p. 85, *Mowlavi*: Persian poet and philosopher of the thirteenth century.

p. 85, *Sar Cheshme*: A square in Tehran.

p. 87, *dervish*: A wandering preacher or holy man.

p. 88, *hadith*: The body of transmitted actions and sayings of the Prophet Mohammad and his companions.

p. 89, *Masnvai*: A famous book of poetry by Mowlavi.